HER FAVORITE HUSBAND
Caron Todd

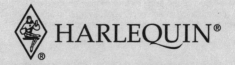

HARLEQUIN®

TORONTO • NEW YORK • LONDON
AMSTERDAM • PARIS • SYDNEY • HAMBURG
STOCKHOLM • ATHENS • TOKYO • MILAN • MADRID
PRAGUE • WARSAW • BUDAPEST • AUCKLAND

ISBN-13: 978-0-373-78259-8
ISBN-10:   0-373-78259-4

HER FAVORITE HUSBAND

CHAPTER ONE

As soon as she saw him, she wanted to feel him inside her. Almost could. It took her breath away. She reminded herself where she was, fourteen hundred miles from home, in a dim cave of a cocktail lounge–frontier saloon, a place decorated with big screen TVs and dead animals. Restraint was called for here.

A waitress walked by, balancing a loaded tray. "Want a table, hon? Help yourself. Anywhere's good."

He turned then, with a disinterested glance at the door, and froze mid-sip of frothy beer. Finished the sip, put down the mug. She couldn't tell if he was only surprised, or also angry. There was no reason to be angry, not after all this time.

She chose the most direct path between the tables that separated them. No leaping up to greet her, she noticed, no sweeping her into his arms. He didn't budge, other than to take a supercasual swig of beer as he watched her weave to his side. She'd come so far, a stone's throw from the arctic circle, and he couldn't even smile?

"Sarah."

"Ian."

"What the hell are you doing here?"

Not only surprised, then. Angry, still.

She climbed onto the bar stool beside his and tried for light-hearted sparkle. "I'm exploring."

"In a skirt and heels?"

"Wrinkle-free fabric." She scrunched a handful of the soft wool-silk blend to demonstrate its Far North worthiness. It was her favorite travel suit, charcoal-gray to show she meant business, with a ruby-red camisole and a small, but real ruby pendant adding not *all* business. She lifted a foot, resting it on one of his. "Close-toed shoes."

"Ah. Practical."

"Always."

He moved his foot out from under hers.

So far, the visit wasn't going very well. What had she expected? Something more. A hug. A bit of delight to go with the surprise.

He looked enticing, if excessively casual, in denims and a navy blue shirt, his hair forming those little curls over his collar the way it did when he put off getting it cut. He sounded enticing, too, his voice as deep as she remembered. All around him, though, was a wall of bristling, possibly antagonistic, energy.

She smiled at the bartender, who smiled back, blue eyes crinkling at the corners. She was tempted to point him out as an example of how to give a friendly greeting. "Could I have a glass of red wine? Something fruity. Beaujolais? A small glass, or I'll get sleepy."

"Dangerous thing for an explorer," Ian said.

Carrying on a light-hearted conversation all by herself wasn't easy. Sarah swiveled from side to side, aware that he noticed the way her skirt tightened as she moved. "Let me say, in the interests of full disclosure and absolute clarity that although in a sense I *am* exploring, I'm not an actual explorer. I'm here because I'm taking a holiday."

"In Yellowknife."

"People do."

"Some people."

"Lots of people."

"Not you."

"You're so sure? What if I've changed?"

"Enough to choose this place for a bedtime drink?"

Her gaze followed his to the moose head over

the bar, then to a mangy bear near the washroom, stretched upright, its mouth open in a silent, toothy roar.

"Which brings me back to my question," he said.

"Why I'm here?" For the first time since yesterday morning, when she'd begun to make her plans, Sarah saw that it was a very good question. *Popped by to see you* was the only answer she had. Popped fourteen hundred miles from home to see him. To see this cold-eyed man. "Do I need a reason to travel?"

She knew what he was thinking. To travel to this particular city, to this particular bar stool, yes, she needed a very good, very sensible reason. Behind his controlled expression, she was sure a fight was brewing. A continuation of the last one, after a ten year pause.

It was hard not to be disappointed. This trip had seemed like the best idea in the world. She'd been so pleased with it she'd hugged it to herself all day long. She must have been imagining an alternate universe, where Ian would love the idea, too, because in this one they never spoke to each other. No birthday calls, no Christmas cards. No hint that either of them would be glad to see the other.

Except, she *had* been glad.

"Of course you don't need a reason." He managed to sound both mild and cold. "It goes without saying you can travel wherever you want. I'm curious about your choice of destination, that's all."

"I've always wanted to see the North. Ever since I first heard about Santa."

It amused her, but there wasn't even a hint of a sparkle in his eyes, nearly black, and shuttered at the moment. And beautiful. Whether they were closing her out or drawing her in as far as she could go, she had always found them beautiful.

"You're annoyed," she said.

"I'm not."

"All this time, and you're still annoyed."

"More like...skeptical."

"All this time and you're still skeptical."

He leaned on one elbow, rotating his beer bottle and watching her. She couldn't believe the distance he was putting between them. How could distrust last so long? She had as much reason to doubt him, but she wasn't giving him the cold shoulder.

The pieces of her plan had fallen together so easily—didn't that mean it was a good one? The stars were aligned, and all that?

The thing was, she'd met someone. Someone kind, handsome, smart, funny. More or less perfect. Of course, any man she liked seemed perfect at first.

Dithering about starting a new relationship was unusual for her, but she felt unsure of herself. Coming here seemed like a chance to get some perspective. Soon she'd be busy with the manuscript of Elizabeth Robb's upcoming book, but right now there was nothing on her desk that Oliver, her partner at Fraser Press, couldn't take care of for her.

Once she'd accepted the idea of getting on a plane, she'd decided to follow a few days in Yellowknife with a trip to Winnipeg. Visiting her parents always settled her down. Then she'd go to Three Creeks, an hour and a half from the city, to encourage and inspire her most bread-winning author. Liz had been disturbingly silent about future projects. That could mean no book the year after next. No one wanted that—not Liz, not her readers and not Fraser Press.

The only imperfect part of the plan was that if Sarah had thought of it a day or two earlier, she could have saved Liz some hefty courier fees and picked up the current manuscript and illustrations in person.

But now, already, the whole alignment thing seemed in doubt.

She looked at Ian, who was busily ignoring

her. They'd only been together for ten minutes. If the visit were a book, this would be the rough draft stage. With some effort, it could still end well.

IAN LOOKED TO THE SIDE one more time. Yup, still there, still her and still looking at him like a kid with a windup toy.

Well, he wasn't going to play.

He knew he was behaving badly. If he could be civil while interviewing poachers who hunted elephants for their ivory, or coffee growers who slashed and burned Amazonian rain forest, couldn't he be civil to Sarah?

A hard knot in his stomach indicated that no, maybe he couldn't.

Saying she had slashed and burned her way through his life might be overdoing it. But she had bashed her way through a year or two of it.

Not that all the memories were bad ones. That made it worse. She'd thrown so much away.

He still couldn't believe she was sitting there as if no time had passed, as if they'd gone out to the pub for the evening. *Beer and darts? Sure, why not?*

Amazing. Sarah, of all people.

She looked good.

She looked lovely.

They'd been kids, more or less, when she'd taken off. Now, she was definitely a woman. Her necklace pointed like an arrow to her cleavage, catching the light and blinking, *this way, this way.*

Statistics weren't his thing, but the probability of the two of them ending up side by side in a Yellowknife bar had to be almost zero.

"Did you call my parents?" he asked. "Someone told you I was here? You're not sick or anything?"

"I'm bursting with health." She smiled, cat that got the cream now that he'd shown concern. Coaxing, looking for a way in. "Does it matter why I came, Ian? We don't have to examine the details, do we? Can't we just go with the flow?"

"I don't think so." Going with the flow had never led to good things.

He leaned against the bar so he could see past her, to one of the televisions on the wall. He'd come down from his room to watch football on the big screen. Bombers versus Argonauts, and after last season, the Bombers had something to prove.

With any luck she'd get bored, and flow someplace else.

IAN SEEMED TO BE WARMING up. At least he'd stopped glaring. Sarah sipped her wine and tried to be unobtrusive while he stared at the TV. After what felt like at least an hour, he made a disgusted sound and turned his back to the screen.

"Am I in the way or are they having trouble catching the ball?"

"Both."

"We could change seats."

He gave her a less unfriendly look than he had so far. "No, thanks. It's pretty clear how the game's going." He moved his mug back and forth on the bar, like someone reconsidering a chess move. "Did you get in this evening?"

"A couple of hours ago." Right away, she'd discovered the first weakness in her travel plan. Yellowknife was bigger than she'd expected, long and narrow, sticking close to the northern shore of Great Slave Lake, and it was full of desk clerks committed to customer privacy. She'd gone from hotel to hotel, hoping to stumble across him in a lobby or coffee shop or lounge.

And she had. Lucky stars, after all.

"You had quite a chunk of the globe to choose from, if you wanted to see the North," he said. "Bit of a coincidence that you walked into this bar."

"Must have been fate." He didn't like fate.

Maybe some tiny part of her was still annoyed, too. Still skeptical.

"You could have gone to Alaska."

"That's true. Nearly straight up from Vancouver, a direct flight. One takeoff, one landing. Much more sensible. You know how I hate takeoffs and landings."

"Or Baffin Island, the Yukon, the Beaufort Sea—"

"I'm not keen on seas, especially cold ones."

"Labrador, the Queen Elizabeth Islands—"

"The who?"

"That big triangle at the top of the continent."

"I've learned something already! My explorations are bearing fruit." She thought she saw a break in his expression, a tiny, tiny ray of amusement, but it quickly disappeared. She looked at him encouragingly, willing him to realize how much fun it was that they should run into each other in a sportsman's bar in the Northwest Territories.

He frowned. So much for her powers of silent persuasion.

"But you chose this spot."

"The Diamond Capital."

His face cleared. "Is that it? You're looking for diamonds?"

"Myself? In the ground, you mean? I'll concede I'm not dressed for prospecting."

Another flicker, suppressed again.

"Anyway, I have enough diamonds."

"Three, I hear," Ian said. "If you count the first."

"Of course I count the first."

"You're not wearing one now."

"The stone was a hazard," she said lightly. She wished he hadn't noticed. "They made me put it in my checked baggage."

"Was your wedding band a hazard, too?"

This wasn't a discussion Sarah wanted to have. After ignoring her for the better part of an hour, did he have to study her so closely now? What did he think he'd see? Pain? Shame? She wouldn't show him either.

"I'm between wedding bands at the moment."

"Between the second and the third?"

"Post-third."

He looked at his beer bottle, long enough, she thought, to read the label five times in both official languages. "That's too bad. You're all right?"

"Of course." At least he didn't seem shocked or titillated by the news, the way some people did. "Puzzled, though. Because here I am, so glad to see you and there you are, so…skeptical."

"You surprised me."

"Which I should never, never do."

At last he smiled, and unexpectedly, it was his old smile—the one she'd wanted to see—warm, kind, much better than the bartender's.

"One second I'm watching a football game and the next you're standing in the doorway. You, of all people…"

"Here, of all places. A ghost. A bad dream. Indigestion."

His chuckle, brief as it was, instantly made her happy.

"None of the above. More of a fold in time."

"Like being catapulted back ten years…"

He'd stopped leaning away from her. Stopped playing with his beer bottle. "Exactly. You came through the door and for a weird millisecond it was like we were back in that dark little apartment on Corydon."

Basement apartment, all they could afford, but handy to the university. "I wish we were." She let her knee bump his in case he missed her point.

"Sarah."

"Don't you wish we were?"

"It was damp, remember? And sometimes we had crickets."

His eyes weren't closing her out anymore. They were drawing her in. It struck Sarah that his coolness until now might not have been disapproval, after all. Not completely, anyway. It might have been an attempt at self-control.

If so, it seemed to be slipping.

She swung the bar stool around, bringing their knees into contact again. Heat flowed right up her leg. She saw when his thoughts went in the same direction as hers—the one place where nothing had ever gone wrong. She laid her hand on his cheek. She didn't know she was doing it until she felt the sharpness of his whiskers.

He stiffened, and for a moment a wall went up. She thought he was going to tell her to take herself, her favorite skirt and her beautiful high heeled shoes all the way back to Vancouver in one giant leap, but he didn't. He didn't say anything.

His hand covered hers. His fingers moved, gentle, exploratory, as if the skin he touched was something unusual, something that needed his full attention. Slowly, down to her wrist, then up again. That was all, but she felt it every-where, in every cell, and from the intensity of his expression, she guessed so did he.

She gave herself a second or two to consider doing the sensible thing. "My hotel is across town. Fortunately, it's a skinny town."

He took more than a second or two, so many seconds she thought he would turn her down. Then he said, "My room's upstairs."

"Even better." She found a ten dollar bill in her purse and put it on the bar. "Unless there's someone who'd rather you didn't?"

"Not lately."

The phrase simmered before her while they walked out of the room, not touching, trying to keep their intentions to themselves. "How lately?"

"Does it matter?"

"No, of course not." They went through the lobby, still tamping down a sense of urgency, nodding to the desk clerk and wishing him a good night. "But is it not lately in the sense of a month or in the sense of a year? Ballpark."

They stepped into the elevator and the doors closed.

"I'm responsible and healthy, if that's what you mean."

It wasn't. Maybe it should have been, but something else was bothering her. As he pressed the button for the third floor she leaned close and spoke against his lips. "I mean, is there anyone else on your mind?" She didn't want there to be, not at the front of it, not at the back, not deep down and half-forgotten.

"You kidding? Sarah's here. All things bright and beautiful."

It took her back, miles and years back, to the week they'd met, to the first time they'd made love. They were dazzled by each other and that was what he'd said to her afterward. *Sarah, all things bright and beautiful.* It was the most poetic thing she'd ever heard, better than in a movie, better than in a book. She'd thought what an angel of a boyfriend she'd found.

But he wasn't an angel at all.

She was standing right against him and each breath brought her chest into contact with his. The tingling made it hard to concentrate. If she took one step away, got just a few inches of air between them, she could think more clearly.

Instead, she moved closer. His arms came around her and they kissed, tentatively at first, feeling their way between past and present.

When the elevator opened they hurried to his room. Door locked, clothes off, skin that was familiar and different at the same time.

She broke away, put her palms on his chest, pushed him onto the bed. She needed that, after all his…skepticism. She needed to be in charge. She liked the way he looked up at her, heated, waiting, visibly struggling to remain passive.

"Anticipation is half the pleasure," she told him.

"Half? Are you sure?"

There was a huskiness in his voice. She could almost feel it against her skin. She got onto the bed, letting her legs rub along his. Somewhere between floor and mattress, waiting became too much for her, too. She lowered herself onto him, gasping at the relief of that touch. Before she'd had time to reconcile the strangeness with the familiarity, heat and a tremulous heaviness gripped her. She gave in to it, and let the waves carry her. In moments, he followed, pulling her hips closer, finding his way deeper, whispering her name.

They rested, and then he began to stroke her again, taking his time, making her feel the way he always had, that there was no one more beautiful or more important to him in all the world. Far at the back of her mind was something she needed to tell him, but she couldn't get hold of it, couldn't see it at all, and soon there were no thoughts left, only him, moving over her and in her, only the rightness of that.

CHAPTER TWO

SHE FELL STRAIGHT TO SLEEP. At first she nestled close, soft puffs of air blowing on his chest. Unbelievable, to feel that again. Soon she turned, onto her side, but with her back still pressed against him. Disconnecting a step at a time.

Soft and sweet as she slept, apparently harmless.

But here, and therefore not harmless.

At the bar he'd nearly walked away from her, even as they'd toyed with the idea of coming upstairs. One foot on the floor, ready to get up and go. That was thanks to a small, really small, portion of his brain that knew what was good for him. They couldn't fall together like this and then just as easily fall away, with no repercussions.

He was an idiot.

Her hair, dark soft waves of it, had fallen forward, a few wisps fluttering each time she exhaled. He propped himself up on one elbow so he could smooth it from her face.

A thinner face. She was thinner all over. *Between wedding bands.* Had three disappointing men taken away her glow, given her those sharper angles? Poor Lady of Shalott. That was what her brothers used to call her. Always dreaming. No real man would ever make the grade.

A few years ago one of their former classmates had told him about marriages two and three. That was when the second was over and the third was on the horizon. *That Sarah. She's had more husbands than I've had winter coats.*

True or not, it wasn't a friendly comment. He'd said so, and got a pitying look. No doubt he was part of the story now. *Poor guy, still on Sarah's hook.*

He would have denied it before that urgent need to get to his room had taken over, before that kick in the chest when he'd turned and seen her at the door.

SARAH WOKE UP RELAXED and refreshed, with no sense of time.

The length of Ian's body was pressed against her back and legs. No one else felt like him. If they'd been apart for fifty years instead of ten, she'd still know who lay behind her. She wished she could doze off again so neither of them would have to move just yet, but she could tell he was awake, too.

"Is it morning?"

He kissed the back of her neck. "You've had a fifteen minute snooze."

"You're kidding." She opened one eye to squint at the window. Natural light glowed around the closed curtains. "So the midnight sun thing is real?"

"At this latitude and time of year, not quite. More of an all-night dusk."

The blanket and sheet had fallen on the floor. Sarah turned onto her back and stretched, happy to have Ian looking at her, confident the years hadn't done her body any harm. "I feel wonderful."

"You sure do."

She nudged him with her hip. "You know what I mean!" His smile made her heart twist. She'd always had a soft spot for him tousled and bleary-eyed.

It wasn't really a happy smile, though.

How could he not be happy, after what they'd shared? They had shared it, hadn't they? She hadn't been on cloud nine all alone while he labored thanklessly?

She rolled onto her side to face him, trying to study him without staring. Already, the drawbridge was on its way back up, his expression becoming guarded, his smile fading.

"Well?" he asked.

"Hmm?"

"Your verdict? My abs okay?"

"More than okay, as you well know!" She stroked the taut skin and felt his muscles tighten. "Much more than okay."

It was an odd feeling, though, to touch him so intimately. Briefly, he'd been her Ian again. Fell asleep, and he was. Woke up, and he wasn't. Like having blurred vision. Then and now, two of him, two of her. Sarah supposed it was to be expected, but it made for a crowded bed.

She pressed her body against his, hoping the feeling would go away. "Wasn't that amazing? How quickly we clicked."

"The question is why."

"Why?" There wasn't any need to ask why. Was it the clicking itself he questioned, or the speed of the clicking?

She couldn't think about it now. Her brain wasn't working on all cylinders. It wouldn't be for hours. Perceptions changed after making love. She'd never figured out if postbliss chemicals cleared the view or clouded it.

"There's a time for thinking, Ian."

"And this isn't it?"

"Of course this isn't it." She leaned over him, running a hand across his chest, then down to those much more than okay abs.

Gently, but firmly, he pushed her away. "I'm still fuzzy about how you landed in Yellowknife."

"Well," she said, watching the space between them grow wider as he sat up and leaned against the headboard, "I think first they pull the rudder back and then they do something with those wing flaps."

"What's the big secret, Sarah? What are you avoiding telling me?"

"There's no secret. I already explained why I came."

"Something about Santa."

"You don't believe I'd search for Santa's workshop?"

His mouth twitched. "You probably would. And now that you spend all your time surrounded by children's books, what could be more natural than an expedition to the North Pole?"

"Hey, you could come along." She was so pleased he knew something about her work. About the rings, too. All these years apart she hadn't been invisible to him. "Take the *National Geographic* photos, write the article. Interview the man himself!"

His attention sharpened when she mentioned his work. "Keeping tabs on me?"

Some self-protective urge got in the way of admitting anything that purposeful. "I wouldn't say tabs."

"What would you say?"

"I'd say—" *I think about you sometimes, I wonder how you are* "—I'd say, I try to notice what's going on around me."

"I haven't exactly been around you."

"The geography isn't the point. You were my first husband. That doesn't go away. There's a little spot in my peripheral vision that is forever yours." She held a finger to one side of her head. "It's about here."

"Pretty much out of sight. I'm surprised you noticed the work I do."

"You're not a spy. You're a photojournalist. It's kind of noticeable. Every now and then a magazine cover pops out at me. Like *Serengeti Safari,* on my way from canned goods to produce."

"You went right by, did you? It stayed on the shelf?"

"Admired, but abandoned, I'm afraid." As soon as she said it she wished she hadn't. It wasn't all that funny. Not terribly diplomatic, either. She hadn't done the abandoning, though.

It was the other way around. He was the one who'd walked out.

"You really just happened to turn up, Sarah? In my hotel?"

Oh, he could be frustrating! She was tired of being interrogated. "After visiting several others."

"Ahh. The coincidence needed help."

Sarah looked around for her purse. It was near the door, half under Ian's jeans. She went to get it, then rejoined him on the bed while she opened it and pulled out a piece of folded newsprint.

"There I was yesterday morning, relaxing in my jammies—"

"Where's 'there,' besides Vancouver?"

"In my apartment. Twelfth floor, oceanside."

"Nice."

"There I was, having my morning coffee and a delicious whole wheat, mega-iced, mega-cinnamon-sugar cinnamon bun, when I opened my weekend paper and found this." She waved the clipping. It was an article describing how gold built Yellowknife in the 1930s and how diamonds under the rock and ice of the Barren Lands were behind another growth spurt now.

"'All That Glitters Isn't Gold.' By Ian Kingsley." She smiled. "I always knew your name would look good in print. This story is why I came to Yellowknife, Ian. You made me want to see the place for myself. At the end you said you'd be here for several weeks, working on a series of columns about the Northwest Territories. So I thought, why not?"

Before she finished speaking, she sensed his withdrawal.

"You dropped everything?" His voice had cooled.

What did that mean? She hadn't dropped anything.

Slowly, she refolded the clipping. "Like a banana peel."

"Right. Of course." He went to the pile of clothes on the floor, purposeful, quick. He was already gone, more or less, before he finished getting dressed. "It's none of my business what you do."

"No."

"Not anymore."

"If it ever was." She couldn't believe what was happening. She'd finally answered his question and now the evening was crumbling, falling apart.

He pulled his shoelaces tight, and tied them with swift, sharp movements. "I'll call you a taxi."

He was throwing her out?

If she'd seen it coming she could have left

first, left him dangling. Nothing to be done about it now. She certainly wasn't going to bob up and down collecting clothes while he watched.

Settling back against the headboard, she turned to give him her left breast's best angle. She could be just as cold as he was. Colder. "I'm not sure it's that easy. You can't say, 'No, thank you' right after, 'Yes, please.' Not if you've accepted what's offered."

"You're right. It's rude. It's unfortunate."

"Do you have a thesaurus? There must be a better word choice." She took her time getting up from the bed, then padded toward him. He seemed unable to stop looking at her, his eyes lingering at all the expected places.

"I'll shower and then we'll talk." That might give him time to settle down, to see that his behavior had gone way past unfortunate to absolutely mean.

But when she came out of the bathroom he wasn't waiting, contrite and ready to apologize. He'd gathered her clothes together and left a note on top of them.

"TAXI'S PAID FOR AND WAITING."

Scribbled under the block capitals was an apparent afterthought. "It was good to see you, Sar."

CHAPTER THREE

TUNNELED UNDER THE covers the next morning, Sarah silently replayed the phrase Ian had used. Good to see her?

He'd actually said that. Written it, anyway, and writing it was worse. He'd had time to tear up the note, time to write a better one.

Good to see her, *Sar.* He'd thrown her out after great sex, and affectionately shortened her name.

How had she landed herself in this mess?

By ignoring a very important prefix, that was how. Ex-wives didn't go to bed with ex-husbands. That was what *ex* meant.

But with Ian, *look, don't touch* had never been an option.

The moment her body had gone into overdrive in that House of Taxidermy they called a bar, she should have headed straight back to the airport, alarm bells ringing.

She couldn't, though. She'd already started

to wonder about her choices where men were concerned, and when she'd seen his photo and byline in the paper her questions had moved front and center. What was she doing, embarking on relationship after relationship? Was it time to try again? Were she and Ian done? Really, forever and truly, done?

An odd thing to wonder after ten years, but the tumbling into bed, the complete and absolute wonderfulness of that, said no.

The turfing out said yes.

Maybe she'd expected too much from one short trip. As if she could stand in front of him and all answers would be revealed. As if he was some kind of oracle.

You dropped everything.

He'd said it so harshly, and cold went the eyes, on went the clothes. Why was he like that, leaping to judgment? "Dropped everything," in that tone, as if she'd abandoned a child or left someone marooned on a cliff. Was that what he thought of her?

She didn't care what he thought of her.

She did care, but she couldn't change it. Couldn't change him.

Muffled through the covers, she heard the room telephone ring.

Ian. She knew it right away. A mortified,

shamed and sorry Ian. Haggard from tossing and turning all night—even more than she had, because he was the guilty one. She had only been unwise.

If he apologized, she would pretend she didn't know what he was talking about. *Note? You're worried about that? Heavens, I was glad to see you, too.*

She reached outside the comforter, felt around on the bedside table for the receiver and with as little banging against clock and lamp as possible, pulled it into her cocoon.

"Hello?"

"Good morning!" The voice on the other end was cheerful and wide-awake, medium deep. Not Ian. Oliver. "What a grumpy sounding woman. It can't be the lovely, vacationing Ms. Bretton."

She threw back the covers to see the clock. Eight? That meant it was seven at home. "Is something wrong? Is Jenny all right?" Jenny was her little mutt, rescued from an animal shelter a couple of years ago and living like a queen ever since. "Oh, Lord, not a car—"

"Jenny's fine," Oliver quickly reassured her. "Missing you, but hale and hearty. She's here by my desk, cocking her head every time you speak."

"Poor girl."

"She's not cocking it sadly. Curiously, that's all." His voice faded and Sarah heard him croon to the dog, saying ridiculous things about it being Mommy on the phone, yes, Mommy, who was far away....

"Stop it, Oliver. You'll embarrass her."

Sarah was coming to grips with two facts— one, that her demon lover hadn't rushed to beg her forgiveness and two, that in another corner of her life she was something other than an idiot. In the eyes of some, in a faraway reno- vated gingerbread house, she was a capable, professional woman.

"What's going on then, if you're both fine? Why are you at work at this hour?"

"Pup needed to go out—did you mention how often and how early her physical needs dominate? I don't think you did—and our walk took us past a coffee shop. Once we had a latte and a double chocolate glaze, there was no going back—"

He broke off, then, with a change in tone, got to the point of his call. "Hate to bother you, Sarah, first day of holidays. There's a compli- cation and I think you'll want to know about it."

She wriggled higher in the bed so she could sit straighter. "What kind of complication?"

"An Elizabeth Robb kind."

There were never any complications from Liz.

"She sent an e-mail this morning at 4:00 a.m. her time," Oliver added, "a panic hour if there ever was one. She claimed she hasn't started the book."

"I know. That's what we're going to talk about when I go to Manitoba. She was bound to get blocked eventu—"

"This year's book," he interrupted.

"What?"

"She hasn't started this year's book."

Sarah got out of bed and paced as far as the phone cord allowed. "The one in the spring catalog?"

"That's the one."

"What does she mean, not started?"

"She means no paintings and no text."

"You're kidding." Liz hadn't said a word about having trouble with this year's book. Although now that Sarah thought about it, she hadn't said the project was going well, either. "Slowly," she'd said, in a don't-bug-me tone. "Does she mean she's not *happy* with the paintings and text?"

"I'm afraid not. I called her as soon as I read the e-mail and asked her to send an attachment of whatever she's done. It isn't even an outline, Sarah. It's doodles."

The news was starting to sink in, but it was

still hard to believe. "Any clue from her about what's wrong?"

"She said there was no book, and went to change a diaper."

"Send me the outline, would you? I'll look at it over breakfast. And Oliver? Give Jenny a hug and a biscuit for me?"

"Already done."

"Thanks. Thanks for taking care of things."

"You'd do the same. You *will* do the same, I promise. Have fun."

"Sure. Always."

Sarah hung up and sat staring at the telephone. Maybe the outline was more complete than it looked at first glance. Maybe an old book could be reissued with added story and illustrations. How about an alphabet book? Liz must have tons of drawings on hand, enough to take a child from A to Z....

The phrase *dropped everything* kept trying to muscle into her thoughts.

IAN PACED FROM THE telephone to the window.

He didn't like feeling in the wrong. She was a grown-up. She made the choices she wanted to make.

He paced some more.

Okay, right. What happened was his choice,

too. Every minute from the time she'd walked into the lounge had been an invitation, but every minute he'd stayed was like saying yes. He couldn't argue his participation had been halfhearted.

It was his hotel. That was the thing to keep in mind. She'd encroached on his territory. Saw the article one day, arrived in town the next… how sensible was that? And for what? To play? He was here to work. Six columns, six weeks. It was a tight schedule and he needed to focus. No distractions, not even Sarah.

Especially not Sarah. They'd written "The End" on their story, not "To Be Continued," not "Tune In Next Decade" for more of the frigging same.

He downed some coffee and a cereal bar, then went through to the shower. If he didn't get a move on he'd be late for his first meeting of the day. He'd booked half an hour with the Mountie who headed the Diamond Protection Service. Cops might be our friends, but annoying them seemed like a bad idea.

When his sluggish brain didn't switch from Sarah's soft, pale skin to interview questions, he turned the tap cooler, then all the way to cold. It woke him up and got him out the door in no time flat.

A COFFEEMAKER SAT ON the desk near the window. Sarah fit a pouch of an unknown roast into the filter basket and filled the reservoir with water. While it dripped, she scanned the file Oliver had sent.

An outline, no. Doodles, yes.

A spot above her eyebrow began to throb. She rubbed it and tried to feel only concern for Liz's welfare. After a book a year for fifteen years—all of which seemed to end up in every library, school and child's bookshelf in the land—what could have happened to sink this one? Painting and writing were Liz's life. They were all she wanted to do.

Or had been, once upon a time long ago and far away. Before she moved back home to Manitoba from Vancouver, before she married her pumpkin farmer, before they started their family. Liz wouldn't be the first woman to sink under the weight of domestic bliss. Clearly, she needed a hand.

When Sarah tried to call she got a busy signal, so she went back to her e-mail program, hoping to catch Liz online. After a couple of false starts in which she either sounded accusing or unreasonably cheerful she typed:

In a bit of a predicament, are you? Don't panic! We're here to help. We'll talk about it more when I see you, but why not give me a head start understanding the problem? Oliver said there aren't any paintings yet. You told me once the images help you see the story. Don't they usually come first?

Sympathetic, she hoped, the question about images a sprinkling of breadcrumbs, the beginning of a path out of the forest. But firm.

By the time she had dressed and put on eyeliner and mascara, there was still no answer from Liz. Sarah took an apple from the side pocket of her suitcase and went out to the balcony, crunching.

She could see the city center, busy with cars and pedestrians. Closer to her, a rocky outcropping extended into a chilly-looking lake. Clusters of small buildings climbed up and down the rock, some apparently teetering on the edge. That must be the Old Town. Ian had written about it, rough shanties built by prospectors during the 1930s gold rush.

To the east, the water went on forever. To the north, beyond the city, green and rust-colored growing things stretched into the distance. In an austere way, it was beautiful.

She couldn't put her finger on what it was about the north that got to her. Not as a direction, not as a place. Maybe, like New York in the song, as a state of mind? It pulled at her. Could it be actual magnetism, the North Pole using its power?

Her worries took a couple of steps back. She wanted to get out there, see the town and the lake close up. Explore, for real.

CHAPTER FOUR

IAN WAS MORE THAN LATE for his appointment. He missed it entirely. He rebooked the interview, for the following day, and went to spend the remainder of the morning at a restaurant that promised authentic northern fare, everything from caribou steak to musk ox burgers to freshly caught Great Slave Lake fish. He ordered bannock and coffee, opened his laptop and tried to work.

Tried but failed.

Sarah had been in his bed. Sarah Bretton Kingsley Bennett Carr. How long would her name be by the time she was fifty? There weren't many decisions he regretted—even the bad ones usually had value—but that "I'll call you a taxi" moment was one. Her face when he'd told her to go…he wouldn't forget that expression in a hurry. And then the way she'd rearranged herself, that sinuous movement that turned her breasts and legs into the only things in the room…

"I'm not sure it's that easy," she'd said, mixing sultry with cool. She was right. The whole uncomfortable scenario of him being wrong about that and her being right about it was complicated by the memory of her leg hooked over his hip. Silky, but insistent.

Taking into account what he knew about Sarah and about the city's hotels, he tried to guess where she'd be staying, if she hadn't already zipped back to Vancouver.

As he guessed, she was registered at the newest, most luxurious place in town. When the switchboard put him through to her room, the answering machine picked up.

"Sarah? It's me." Although there weren't many customers in the restaurant, he lowered his voice as he said, "Don't know about you, but I didn't get much sleep last night. My behavior—"

What could he say about his behavior?

"It was inexcusable." Strong word. He felt better, saying it. "Pretty much from hello. You probably know what happened. Same old problem, right? One of them, anyway."

He understood the banana peel remark had been an exaggeration, but it was true enough. Sarah jumped into things without looking, and she thought it was a good quality.

"That's no excuse," he added, wishing he hadn't brought up the past. Blaming the other person had a way of watering down an apology. "I was a jerk no matter what the provocation. Anyway, I'm sorry for being thoughtless last night. And I hope you're okay this morning."

He imagined her voice, teasing, amused, saying of course she was all right. He used to wonder if it was even possible to hurt her. It was easy to infuriate her, but most of the time she kept things light. Or sexy. Like last night, walking toward him naked, as if he'd be mesmerized and do whatever she wanted.

As if? She'd nearly got her wish.

"I have to go, Sarah. Maybe I'll see you again sometime."

As soon as he ended the call he realized he shouldn't have left it open-ended. He should have said goodbye. None of that till we meet again stuff. A definite we're done goodbye.

That's what it was in his mind. Always had been.

He woke up his sleeping laptop. In one pane, he began playing a downloaded video that showed how diamonds formed. In another, he typed Column, Week Two.

Diamonds are forged by intense heat and pressure deep in the earth's mantle....

Boring. Delete.

Diamonds are almost as old as the world itself. Some say they come from the stars....

Boring and vague. Delete.

He tried again.

The only diamond that ever caught my fancy was small and flawed, but that imperfect fraction-of-a-carat held a whole world, a whole future.

He stared at that for a while, then deleted it, too.

SARAH'S SPIRITS BEGAN TO rise as soon as she felt the sun on her face. Last night couldn't be undone. The problem of the missing book couldn't be solved, not today, not until she and Liz sat down together. All she wanted from this moment in time was to take it in, to see and hear and smell it.

For a small city, Yellowknife bustled. Ian had talked about that in his column, about people coming from all over the world to work in the diamond industry. Walking along the sidewalk, she heard so many languages spoken it was like an outdoor United Nations. The speakers of those languages were mostly men. Young, strong men of the wood-chopping, diamond-digging variety.

She hadn't planned to shop, but all along her

route to the Old Town the stores were filled with local arts and crafts. She found treasures every few steps—soapstone carvings, photographs of the summer's never-setting sun and the winter's northern lights, traditional beaded leatherwork and incredible quilts with colorful, hand-sewn northern scenes. Soon she had souvenirs for everyone in her family and at Fraser Press, and had moved on to birthday and Christmas presents.

Just when she thought she couldn't carry another thing, she came to a bookstore. Bookstores, she'd always thought, were as good as a rest, so she opened the door with her two free fingers and stepped inside.

"Oh, my goodness," a woman said, hurrying from behind a counter. "Let me help you with those packages." For a moment they were almost bound together, trying to untangle bags without dropping any. "Have you bought the entire town?"

"Not yet, but there's still tomorrow." Sarah pulled her collar away from her throat, letting a breath of air reach her skin. Her sweater, hand-knitted Peruvian alpaca wool, had seemed perfect when she was packing. "I didn't think to check the weather before leaving home. It's summer."

"Yes, it is. For a while. A short, but delightful while. You're not the first to think we have winter year-round." The clerk didn't seem to mind Sarah's ignorance. She had a grandmotherly manner. Sarah could imagine her curling up with a child, getting comfortable to read a story. "Feel free to browse and if you see something you'd like to buy, I'll be happy to send it to wherever you're staying."

Sarah thanked her, and turned to see the display on the closest table. It was a collection of children's books. J. K. Rowling, C. S. Lewis, Enid Blyton…and Elizabeth Robb.

The familiar covers jumped out at her. There was an early story about a boy and a space pirate, a more recent book about warring fairies—Liz had written that one while falling in love with Jack—and a third, Sarah's favorite, a nature book, all lush paintings and no text, done in memory of Liz's first husband.

She began to leaf through it. Andy was on every page, a boy discovering the variety of life in a forest.

The clerk must have noticed her interest. "That one is by a Manitoba author. Very popular. What's the age of the child in question?"

"Oh, about thirty," Sarah said, with a laugh. "But I already have these three. I'm enjoying remembering the first time I read them."

"They're lovely books, aren't they? So colorful, and full of warmth, I always think. Robb has another book coming out in the spring. We've started a sign-up sheet."

"You need a sign-up sheet?"

"It saves disappointment. I wouldn't say the response compares to Harry Potter, but we do get a stream of parents and children coming in the month of an Elizabeth Robb release."

That was good news and bad news. "I'll keep an eye out for it." A desperate, anxious eye.

Sarah chose some books—biographies of northern explorers and prospectors—and carried them to the checkout counter. As if the reminder of Liz's problem wasn't enough, taped to the wall behind the cash register she saw a clipping of Ian's column. His black-and-white photo stared back at her.

I didn't, she wanted to tell it. *I didn't drop anything.*

ALL RIGHT, SO SHE had been a little careless where Liz was concerned. That don't-bug-me tone had merited closer attention. Oliver could lecture her about it if he wanted, but not Ian.

With heavy bags digging into her fingers and banging against her legs, she finally came to the lake. On a map or from the air its shape made her think of a goose in flight. From the ground, it was like an ocean. The water went on and on, all the way to the horizon, clear and blue and sparkling.

Brightly painted houseboats—blue, red, yellow—were tethered on the north side. Farther out, sailboats and windsurfers glided across the waves. A few hardy people were swimming. In spite of the sun, the nearly twenty-four-hour sun, she couldn't believe it was warm enough for that.

It reminded her of the Whiteshell, where her family had a cottage. Huge sheets of weathered granite sloped up from the lake. Along the shore, rocks had long ago broken off and tumbled into the water. A stab of homesickness struck her.

"Kinda pretty, a'nit?"

Sarah turned with a start to see an old man nearly at her elbow. She stepped back, more comfortable having a few feet between them, even though he seemed too frail to do any harm. He wasn't a hundred percent clean. As soon as she noticed that she felt guilty.

"I didn't hear you," she told him.

He raised his voice. "Pretty, a'nit?"

She smiled, not sure if he was joking. "I meant I didn't hear you coming."

"Ah." He nodded. "You was off in your own world. From away, are ya?"

"Vancouver. And you're from here?"

He jerked a thumb over his shoulder. "From the Flats."

He must mean Willow Flats, part of the Old Town. Sarah wondered if he was one of the prospectors who'd built there during the Depression. That would make him, what, ninety-five? Couldn't be. Maybe he'd come during the second wave of gold mining. That would put him in his seventies or eighties. From the look of him he hadn't had much luck, whatever brought him here.

"I'm taking my walk," he told her. "Up to the caf for a beer."

"In the morning?" She couldn't help asking.

"Be noon once I'm there."

The café, looking out over the water from the other side of the narrow peninsula, *was* a long walk for a slow-moving old man. Sarah wondered if she should offer him a few dollars. She didn't want to offend him, but here she stood with bags and bags of souvenirs, and there he wobbled in his dusty clothes.

"I don't suppose you'd let me buy you that beer?" She felt in her pocket and brought out a few five dollar bills, enough for a meal, as well. "To thank you for stopping to make me feel welcome?"

"Well, ya know, I did that for free." He nodded in farewell and started away, leaving her with her hand and the bills outstretched.

Embarrassed, she put the money back in her pocket. She didn't seem to be doing much right lately.

Not far along the shoreline was a place where the stones were terraced like stairs. They led to a flat rock shelf big enough for a few people to sunbathe. She tucked her purchases into a dry, shaded nook, put her shoes on top, rolled up her slacks and waded into the lake.

Cold, clear water lapped over her toes, then over her ankles. It chilled her through, an odd sensation when she was so hot, like chills and fever. Minnows and water bugs darted to her feet, then away. She stopped to watch a small plane take off, slapping against the water before it lifted to the air and headed north, its loud engine fading to a drone.

She reached the stone steps and she climbed onto the shelf. There was one just like it at her family's cottage. She and her brothers had fished from it, dived from it, had campfires on it. She and Ian had made love on it, late at night when there was a new moon, so nothing but stars lit their bodies.

The good memories were the ones that gave

her the most trouble. Better memories than she had with anyone else.

Right from day one.

First class, first day of university, Old English lit, two rows ahead and three seats over. The cutest guy on the face of the earth.

Of course, at that point she hadn't seen many guys yet.

Beowulf, as fascinating as he was, had receded. Her world, in that moment, was composed only of herself and this unknown boy. She was sorry for everyone else, everyone who wasn't her, about to fall in love with him.

They had nearly all their classes together. That first week, she didn't learn a thing. Didn't take a single note. Didn't turn a page. She watched Ian.

He was different from anyone she'd met before. Quiet, still, but not from shyness. She could tell it was from listening and thinking so intently.

One day they went for coffee and he talked about Shakespeare the way other guys talked about video games—like something vivid and fun, full of muscled, sweaty men with swords, not English actors in tights.

She couldn't concentrate on what he said, though. All she could think was that she wanted to kiss him. She watched his face and his eyes, watched them change as his thoughts changed, noticed the way his mouth tightened when he stopped to think, and the way his lips parted and softened when he spoke. She thought of the way her lips would feel on his.

One day she did it. Kissed him. Right there in the coffee shop. What she hadn't imagined was the heat, the current, sparked by that touch. It propelled them, no questions asked, into his dorm room and onto his bed.

They spent days in his room. Shakespeare was still in the mix. With Ian, Shakespeare was always part of it. Of course, Sarah was a fan, too. After seeing an old video of the Olivia Hussey *Romeo and Juliet,* how could she not be? But for Ian the *Complete Works* was like a self-help book. Shakespeare, Ian had claimed, understood everything, all human yearnings, all the mistakes and all the dreams.

Sarah didn't want to think what the Bard would say about her now, a comic character on a fool's errand to Yellowknife. Never mind rose-colored glasses; the minute she'd read that article on Saturday morning, she'd put on a blindfold.

THE WALK BACK TO THE hotel was uphill all the way. By the time Sarah reached the New Town, she felt as old and tired as the man by the lake.

She stopped for a breather, and saw three restaurants within close range. A pizzeria straight ahead, a Chinese establishment at one end of the street and a place that claimed to serve authentic northern fare down the other.

She went closer to read the menu posted on an outside wall. There through the window was Ian, like a framed picture, lost in thought, a cup of coffee beside his laptop.

Writer at Work. No, that didn't fit. He didn't look productive at all. *Stalked by Guilt?*

Probably not. By now he'd managed to squeeze the mistake he'd enjoyed so much into some dark, unused corner of his brain, then shut the door and locked it.

The imbalance between them unsettled her. He so clearly didn't want to see her, but she wasn't done needing to see him.

It was noon and she was hungry. She decided to go in.

CHAPTER FIVE

SARAH MANEUVERED HERSELF and her bags onto the bench seat across from Ian's and gave him a bright smile. "You don't mind, do you? I've been shopping all morning and I'm starving."

She couldn't tell if he minded or not. He closed his laptop and pushed it to one side, then caught a waiter's eye, pointed at his coffee cup and signaled for another.

At least his first move wasn't to call a taxi.

His water glass, apparently untouched, sat a tantalizing few inches away from her. "Could I have that? I'm parched."

"Help yourself."

"Another half hour out there and I'd be dead from dehydration." The restaurant was busy, but not full. From the door she hadn't seen the empty tables. She'd only seen Ian.

She drank most of the water, then patted some on her forehead. The coolness was such a relief she spooned out a few small ice cubes and dropped them inside her sweater. "This is the Arctic, right? I didn't take a wrong turn and end up in Arizona?"

"It's the subarctic—"

"Oh, the *sub*arctic."

"And you're dressed for fall."

He was dressed for gardening, or fishing, something outdoorsy, a bit casual even for a free-lancer. The look suited him—the open collar, the rolled up sleeves, the signs of a little too much sun and just the right amount of muscle.

Her body began to tingle. Apparently it had no IQ at all.

"I thought you might be on your way home by now," Ian said.

"That would have been a very short holiday."

"You're staying?"

"Hard to accept, is it?"

"No, no…of course not. You should enjoy the sights."

The sentence sounded incomplete. Enjoy the sights quickly, he was saying, leave town even faster.

He had already ordered his meal. By the time the waiter arrived with coffee, Sarah had chosen one of the lunch specials printed on a blackboard menu—an almost zero-fat meal of poached arctic char and a salad.

When the waiter left she said, "Ian, could we let it go?"

"It?"

The unpromising response made her pause. "Whatever's causing problems between us."

He looked the way he had yesterday, withdrawn, and not friendly in the least. It was hard to feel good about the middle part of the evening given his antagonism before and since.

Oh, well. She'd unmade the bed, and regardless of lumps, she'd have to lie in it for a while.

The slight variation on the old saying made her smile, and a man two tables over smiled back. It cheered her up. Male admiration had a way of putting a spring in her step.

"Careful, Sarah."

"Of?"

"Some of the men around here are just down from the mines. They're two weeks in, two weeks out."

"Not exactly an eternity."

"They spend half the month in a high-security zone accessible only by plane in summer and ice road in winter. The other half of the month they like to unwind—"

"Understandably. It's nice of you to be concerned, but it isn't necessary. What do you think I've been doing for the past ten years?"

"Getting married, apparently." He muttered it almost grumpily. His tone surprised Sarah. Pleased her, too.

"Looking after myself. Spying the wolves with my own little eye. Anyway, if I were looking for romance there's someone at home who—"

His shock stopped her. A flash of it, then nothing, his face expressionless.

He'd misunderstood. And thought the worst.

The waiter arrived with their meals. They sat in stiff silence while he deposited plates in front of them and refilled their coffee cups.

She wouldn't explain. Let Ian leap to his regularly scheduled judgments.

"SOMEONE AT HOME." Ian tried to keep his voice neutral.

"That's right."

Maybe in her book, cheating with an ex wasn't really cheating. He'd thought better of her.

"How many winter coats have you had since we broke up?"

"How many?" She looked at him blankly. "I have no idea."

"It's been ten years. Three coats? Four?"

She shrugged. "I have a long gray one with a fur collar for formal occasions. A red one for dreary days. A ski jacket for the slopes. A black-

and-white houndstooth for contrast when I wear all black. An all-weather trench with a zip-out lining. A long down parka for visiting at home in January. A cape, but that's not strictly a coat—"

"Okay. Got it."

"Got what?"

"You have a coat for every mood and every occasion." Maybe he was finally starting to understand her. "This is just the way you are, isn't it?"

"I don't know. What am I agreeing with?"

"Your need for variety."

She picked at her fish, separating the flakes with her fork. After a few moments she said, "This is very good char."

Ignoring an idea she didn't like, as usual.

Just as well. He was starting to feel ashamed of himself, being petty enough to ask the question.

They went on talking, two acquaintances catching up on each other's news. About parents and siblings, about the storm that had destroyed her family's house a couple of years earlier. Ian had heard about it at the time. It was a real loss. A grand old house, moldering away until the wind gave it a swift end. He'd liked the place. Missed it, after the divorce. Missed her family, too.

"Why are you pretending you're not angry, Sarah?"

"Angry?"

"About last night."

She gave him a cool smile. "You think I can't have a roll in the hay and come out of it unscathed? It didn't mean all that much to me, Ian. And your…behavior wasn't a big surprise. It's what you do."

"What I do?"

"Run off."

"*I* run off?"

Their voices had steadily been getting louder. Not much, but people at nearby tables had noticed. He lowered his, and suggested that she should, too. Even before he'd finished saying it, the anger he'd known must be there swept into her face.

"DON'T TELL ME HOW LOUDLY to speak. You're the one who can't carry on a normal conversation. And then you *scold* me?"

Ian pushed his plate away. "I don't need this, Sarah. We've been divorced for ten years. There has to be some advantage to that, right? Lunches don't have to dissolve into fights anymore."

"Our lunches never dissolved into fights.

What are you talking about? Is that how you remember it?"

"It doesn't matter how either of us remembers it. We were married for two years a decade ago. A blip in both our lives."

A blip? "And last night? Was that a blip, too?"

"Of course it was."

"A blip."

"Had to be, didn't it?"

She was annoyed, for no good reason. She knew he was right.

It was the physical thing. They'd gone to bed the week they met and after that they had tumbled together at every opportunity. As hello, as goodbye, as good-morning and good-night. As an apology. As exercise. As entertainment. Anytime they got within three feet of each other. They'd mistaken it for belonging together.

"I don't mean to be offensive," Ian said. "It was one time only. By definition that's a blip."

"Why are you going on and on about it? You're protesting a little too much. The blipness of last night getting to you?"

He took a few bills from his wallet, tucked them under his cup, stuck his laptop into its case and started out of the restaurant.

She wasn't going to be left behind, not again.

Loading up her parcels, she hurried outside, too. By the time she reached the sidewalk he was half a block ahead, waiting at the curb for the light to change.

Just as it did, she caught up with him. He crossed the road and turned right. That was the direction she'd come from in the morning, so she went that way, too, nearly stepping on his heels.

He responded by taking bigger steps. Over his shoulder he said, "Sarah, I have work to do."

"So do I."

"Work?"

"Sure. What did you think, that I dropped everything? I'm in contact with the office. A big, fat, profit-draining problem has already landed on my lap."

"Then why don't you stop following me?"

"What makes you think I'm following you? How arrogant is that?"

"You're behind me, going in the same direction."

"Whither thou, darling."

"It's a bit late for that."

Sarah gave an exasperated groan. "Honestly, your sense of humor could fit on a flea! I'm not following you. You're not the center of everything, you know. I'm going to my hotel."

He pointed behind them. "Your hotel's that way."

She swung around, ready to argue, but there it was, the tallest building around, easy to see if only she'd looked.

"Come on, I'll take you."

"I don't need you to take me!"

He ignored her, his whole body expressing his aggravation. He couldn't be half as aggravated as she was, because now she really was following him.

He stopped in front of the hotel's big double doors. "Okay?"

"It was okay before. And just so you know, I don't like you when you're sarcastic."

His irritation seemed to evaporate and he looked at her with something approaching gentleness—tanned, hard-edged gentleness. It completely threw her. "I'm sorry, Sarah."

As soon as he said it she was sorry, too, although she didn't know exactly why and, in any case, wasn't willing to say so.

"What a pair we are." He checked his watch, muttered that he was late, and headed back down the street.

CHAPTER SIX

SARAH EASED HER PACKAGES out of her arms and onto the bed, then pulled off her sweater, relieved to feel cool air on her skin.

Nobody made her angry the way Ian did. It was as if she had a hidden switch only he could find and flick on. It never stayed on for long, though.

The telephone's message light was blinking. She lifted the receiver and pressed the retrieval button.

"You have—one—message," the robotic voice said. "Nine—forty-five—a.m." After a click, she heard Ian's voice.

"Don't know about you, but I didn't get much sleep last night." There was a pause, long enough for her to slip off her shoes and sit on the side of the bed. When he continued, she was surprised how genuinely disappointed in himself he sounded. At lunch, he hadn't seemed sorry or disappointed at all.

Then he ruined it, talking about same old problems and provocations.

Still, it was nice that he'd tried.

Why hadn't he told her in the restaurant that he'd called? Nine-fifty, soon after she'd left the hotel. She wouldn't have been angry at lunch if she'd known about the message. Not very angry, anyway.

"We aren't good together," she told the wall. "Simple as that."

SARAH CHANGED INTO LIGHTER clothes and began to pack the presents she'd bought. There was no way they'd all fit in her luggage. She'd have to send most of them home by mail.

A few things could take the place of the wine she'd brought with her. She set the bottle on the desk. It was a Grand Cru burgundy, meant to celebrate a special occasion. She'd pictured drinking it under the northern lights while belugas leaped out of the sea.

Belugas were a long way from Yellowknife, though, and it turned out northern lights and midnight sun couldn't happen at the same time. Who knew?

Her laptop beeped. A message had come in. Sender, Liz McKinnon. Aka Elizabeth Robb.

Not this time.

Sarah had to scroll down to remind herself what she'd said that morning. It was a question about images coming before text.

Not this time? That was it? Where was the explanation? The urgency? The realization that faraway bookstores were already lining up readers?

Instead of typing HOW COULD THIS HAPPEN?, the uppercase letters denoting a shout, Sarah confined herself to asking,

What's different this time?

Liz's answer arrived ten minutes later.

I'm married. I'm a mother. I'm a Wife and Mother.

Sarah understood. New commitments, busier days. That didn't mean her old commitments had disappeared.

Poor Liz! Things not going well?

A few minutes passed.

This place should be called Robbtown. More people come in and out of the house than I ever saw in Vancouver—to talk to, anyway—and almost all of them are relatives who think because I'm at home I'm not working. Then there are the diapers.

It was hard to imagine Liz dealing with diapers. Hard to imagine anyone dealing with them.

I'm sorry about the crowds of Robbs. Sorry about the diapers, too.

Sarah hesitated before adding to the message. Should she ease Liz along or drag the monster out of the closet and, she hoped, see how puny it really was?

Drag out the monster, she decided.

We'll talk about this more when I see you, but I'm wondering...do you need to postpone the book? Cancel it?

The answer came immediately.

No. No! I'll figure it out. Sorry, Sarah, but I've got to go. Baby's crying, kettle's whistling, dog's barking. See ya.

Sarah tried not to be irritated by the casual sign-off.

The monster didn't look all that puny. Liz either couldn't or didn't want to ignore the distractions her life was throwing at her.

If her book wasn't finished in time there'd be an empty spot in the company's catalog and an empty spot on bookstore shelves, one another publisher would be glad to fill.

Sarah rubbed her eyes. Her head was starting to throb. So much for taking a break and getting perspective. Surrounded by tundra and houseboats and Old Town shanties and she hardly had a chance to—

Of course…why hadn't she thought of it right away? She hurried to the phone and dialed Liz's number.

No answer. That was always the way with Liz. The phone was busy, or no one was there. With an e-mail, an answer could take hours, even a whole day.

Liz, I told you, didn't I, that I'd be in Yellowknife before Manitoba? That's where I am now. You've got to come. Instead of me going to you, you come here. Every two steps you'll trip over a story. You can't be here and not see pictures. You'll have to hurry, though. I'm flying back to Vancouver on the weekend. I know it's rushed, but it'll be worth it. All right?

Every few minutes Sarah hit the receive button. Nothing happened. With any luck, it meant Liz was hard at work. Off in the woods with her easel and paints. Or shut in the attic, insulated from interruption.

Finally, Liz answered.

I'm a Wife and Mother. Did you forget?

Uh-oh, Sarah thought, this time noticing the capital letters. Liz wasn't just overwhelmed. She had a martyr complex in the making. Sympathy would be the worst thing to offer.

Hand infant to husband. Point nose north. Flap wings.

For half an hour, Sarah heard nothing back. She heated water through the coffeemaker, directly onto a tea bag in a mug. She dipped the bag in and out, burned her tongue on the first sip and wished she had her own kitchen with a proper kettle, a nice porcelain pot and a wide choice of premium tea leaves.

The laptop dinged.

Infant handed. Flight booked. Arriving Yellowknife Thursday.

Like magic, Sarah's headache began to subside.

The schedule would still be tight; there was no getting away from that. But a few days here, and Liz would have grist for the mill for years to come.

CHAPTER SEVEN

SARAH RESERVED THE room adjoining hers for
Liz and spent the rest of the afternoon prepar-
ing it as she would at home, with magazines, a
tin of mints, a basket of fruit and chocolate, and
teas and coffees to augment those supplied by
the hotel.

By evening, the long, complicated day had
caught up with her. She bought a sandwich
from the hotel coffee shop and took it up to her
room. She wanted bubbles, cocoa, a book and
her dinner, all in the tub.

First, she would return Ian's call, so she
could forget about him and his odd apology.

She undressed with one hand and dialed his
hotel with the other. The front desk connected
her and the answering machine came on.

"Got your message, Ian. Thanks. You said
you supposed I knew what happened last night.
Actually, I don't know. Pretty much from bar
to bed to goodbye. It feels wrong to be grumpy

with each other, though, doesn't it? Do you want to meet for a drink tonight?"

The question had slipped out. If she could have caught it and put it back in her mouth, she would have. She didn't want a drink. Not with him, not with anyone. She wanted a bubble bath and bed. Besides, an innocent drink was how the previous evening had begun.

Since she couldn't take back the suggestion, she added, "Not as a prelude to anything, just a drink. I want to think we can be civil to each other. For old time's sake."

She liked the sound of that. Postbliss and postfight chemicals had nothing to do with the invitation. "Anyway, I'll be here for a while if you want to give me a call."

SARAH HELD HER BOOK SAFELY above the bubbles. She had just finished reading about a young man from Ontario who'd gone north to find his fortune during one of the 1880s gold rushes, and had never been heard from again. He'd simply disappeared.

The cold could have got him, she supposed. A glacier. Wild animals. Rapids. Other gold-seekers. The book was full of similar stories about southerners with a dream coming up against the harsh realities of the north. It was different now, with modern travel and technology. Safer.

Sarah let the book fall to the floor, and slid deeper into the bubbles. She wished she hadn't fought with Ian today. He was her harsh reality, always insisting on being unreasonable.

They used to get along. There weren't any lunches that dissolved into fights. Ian had to be thinking of someone else. She remembered lunches much differently. Sexy lunches, study lunches, long, wonderful conversation lunches.

Once, at exam time, with books and binders open all over the apartment, and stress oozing from the walls, she'd looked up from her notes and thought again how absolutely beautiful he was. But upset. He was studying for his one science credit and had been afraid he would fail.

She'd gone over to commiserate with him. Had ruffled his hair and told him he should grow it longer. He'd said his dad would just cut it off.

"Between visits home, then." He was from Churchill, on the coast of Hudson Bay, too far by train and too expensive by plane, so visits home were few and far between. "You'd look like Shelley—"

"Please. Blond, ruffly and hooked on opium?"

"Byron, then. One of those tragic Romantic guys. You've got the somber stare—"

"Somber?"

"You don't like somber? It makes me weak-kneed, sweetheart."

"I love somber."

She touched his lips, his nose, his chin, describing how handsome they were. When she reached his forehead she said, "That big, brainy brow," and he'd interrupted, young enough, she now realized, to be afraid he looked peculiar.

"Oh, thanks. Now I'm a Neanderthal." He pronounced it oddly to her ear, with *t* instead of a *th* sound.

"*Brainy* brow. What's wrong with having Neander*tal* ancestors? Don't you hope they've left a trail of genes in some of us?" She climbed onto him and held a strand of her long hair across his forehead to make one shaggy eyebrow. "See, they rise again, my brilliant cave boy."

Keeping the hair in place over his eyes involved a lot of wriggling and tickling, and soon she exclaimed, "Oh! They *do* rise again," and the two of them had rolled, laughing, onto the floor.

Their lunches didn't dissolve into fights.

IAN HAD SPENT THE afternoon finalizing details for a trip into the Barren Lands. From what he'd heard of the area it was mostly deserted, a huge region of rock and water. The treeline zig-zagged through it and caribou migrated across it. He got the impression the dominant species were mosquitoes and biting flies. Sounded just like home.

He went to the bedside telephone to check for messages. There was one. From Sarah.

Why would she suggest a drink? What did she want, anyway?

To sightsee. That couldn't be all. She wanted something from him.

Maybe it was about unfinished business. Their marriage had ended suddenly. He'd gone around with a "Hey, wait a minute," feeling for months. Maybe she had, too.

This wasn't months, though. It was years. Did they still have loose ends to tie up? The Sarah he knew wouldn't bother with something like that. Full steam ahead, damn the torpedoes. And the wedding vows.

He didn't understand her. At lunch she'd barely referred to the night before or to his apology. She'd been friendly, sort of, but got angry in no time flat. Why sit at his table, why bother, if she was mad at him? Why not ignore him? That's what he'd do.

He almost wanted to call her to say, "Look, what's going on?"

But she wouldn't tell him, would she? She'd say nothing was going on, that she'd flown from her bed in Vancouver to his in Yellow-knife, but that it didn't mean anything because she'd always wanted to visit the North, anyway. Oh, right, and by the way, there was someone waiting for her at home. Having sex was some sort of accident, whoops, pardon me, now let's get back to the itinerary, lunch and shopping.

Was it just too easy for her to attract men, so she picked them up and dropped them without much thought? Short attention span? Couldn't say no, no matter how many proposals she heard and in spite of any preexisting husbands? And if attracting men was so easy, why had she jumped back into *his* bed?

Of course, she hadn't done it alone. He'd jumped, too. As always. If they could have con-ducted their lives from under the covers they'd still be together.

The confusing thing was that when she'd walked into the lounge last night and the res-taurant today, he'd been glad to see her. That didn't make sense, when he still had all this deep-down anger. Hanging on to the anger didn't make sense, either.

He'd never met a more frustrating person than Sarah. Impractical, often thoughtless, but from the start he'd been drawn to the light in her, to the impression she gave of always being close to laughter, to the way she jumped whole-heartedly into whatever she did. That was the thing about Sarah, her enthusiasm.

It could go the other way; she could be just as enthusiastically pissed off. Or just as enthu-siastic about some other guy. No use asking her to focus her smile more narrowly or to save her displeasure for someone else.

This was how it was going to be for a while. Every train of thought would change direction and head straight for Sarah. It had been hard, learning not to do that. Took a couple of years.

He went to the window and looked out at the tall rectangle of her hotel. Her message was a few hours old, but she'd said she'd be there for a while, if he wanted to call.

Did he want to? No. No, he didn't.

CHAPTER EIGHT

COMING INTO THE HOTEL lobby from what she promised herself was one last visitor-supply trip, Sarah saw Ian loitering by a potted plant. She told herself his presence might have nothing to do with her. He might be waiting to interview a source in the coffee shop.

Then he left the potted plant and came to meet her.

"I didn't think I'd see you again," she said.

"Were you hoping not to see me?"

"I don't know what I was hoping. You look tired."

"Two sleepless nights. I figure my conscience is trying to tell me something."

"Any idea what?"

"Something along the lines of…I haven't been very nice to you."

She could have told him that. People needed to learn things for themselves, though. He sounded so sheepish, she had to smile.

"So I came to apologize," he said.

"Again?"

"Well, there's the abject kind of apology and the grudging kind. Sleep may be holding out for abject."

"I'm not."

"No?"

"Of course not. Just the sincere kind. Anyway, I haven't been an angel myself." She hesitated. How often could she extend a hand before one or both of them thought she was pathetic? "I'm getting ready for company. Want to come up?"

"To your room?"

"Yes, to my room. We can behave ourselves, can't we? Sit in chairs, talk the way people do."

"Maybe not. There's nice and then there's pushing it. I'd rather we kept things unemotional."

"You don't think we can if we're alone?"

"I know we can't. Anyway, I have an appointment. Already missed it and rescheduled it once. Three appointments, really. A Mountie, the mining claims recorder and a gem cutter. It's going to be a busy afternoon."

"I'd love to see a gem cutter at work. Mind if I tag along?" Like the drink offer last night, the question was out before she could stop herself.

"He's not doing a demonstration. He's only showing me some rough. If I say yes, then are we even? Nothing from the past couple of days will come back to bite me?"

She pretended to think about it. "Deal."

Ian looked at his watch. "Ten minutes? I'll pick up some coffee. Dark roast, black?"

"Wonderful." Sarah hurried up to her room to put away her purchases.

Something had changed during the conversation. Ian's feelings were even more mixed than hers, and much more negative but just now the scales had tilted. She'd felt them tilt.

She combed her hair, touched up her lipstick, changed her shoes and searched through her roll-up jewelry bag. Since they were going to visit a gem cutter, she chose her biggest and best engagement ring.

Her hand hovered over the ring Ian had given her. It was tiny, but pretty. To buy it he'd dropped two classes for the refund, and worked extra hours at a car wash. The day he'd proposed and put it on her finger she'd felt swept off her feet, into some sort of cloudless never-never land. Of course, she'd known there'd be trouble at times, but she'd never thought there'd be enough trouble to ruin everything.

A gold chain was looped through the ring. Sometimes she wore it around her neck, because it was part of her history. Because it was the first.

This afternoon, wearing it felt right. She fastened the clasp, and tucked the chain and ring under her blouse.

IAN WAITED UNTIL THEY were on the sidewalk, then handed Sarah a disposable cup. "Sumatran roast, extra dark, extra large."

When she reached to take it, he saw the ring on her finger. Ring finger, left hand. A large diamond rising from its setting to catch the light.

He started walking in the direction of the RCMP detachment. Had she patched things up with the third husband? Or had the someone at home popped the question since she'd called Ian about drinks yesterday?

One of them must be the company she expected.

Maybe this time things would work out better for her. That would be great. He'd be happy for her if she could get settled, content.

That wouldn't be what she wished for herself. He had no idea what she was looking for as she went through husbands, but it sure wasn't contentment.

"Are we late?" she asked breathlessly. "If I'd known we'd be jogging I might not have taken the coffee."

"We're fine." He slowed down, but had trouble keeping to a pace that let either of them sip their drinks.

She tucked a hand through the curve of his arm. "Relax, then. Enjoy the coffee. Chat."

He didn't want to chat. He didn't want her hand on his arm.

"I forgot," she said. "This is a workday for you. Do you need to concentrate? I can be quiet, enjoy the sights, soak up the ambience."

She proceeded to do it, sort of, sipping and humming her way toward downtown, muttering every now and then about the freshness of the air, the view, the sound of floatplanes taking off or landing in the harbor.

Everything he thought of saying was ridiculous. *Don't wear that teasing expression all the time. Stop having shiny hair. Don't radiate whatever it is you radiate.*

They said if an alcoholic had a drink years after quitting, it landed him right back where he'd started. That's what being around Sarah was doing to him.

Day at a time, then.

"Sarah, how long did you say you're staying?"

"A few more days. Why?"

"Your business will survive?"

"Of course. Oliver's the best partner in the world and we have a good team working with us."

Was Oliver the someone? "You mentioned a problem that's worrying you, a big, profit-draining problem."

"I can worry anywhere. Like being ambidextrous."

Maybe this Oliver person did the worrying and Sarah's contribution was taking authors to lunch.

"And is Yellowknife all the north you want to see?"

"It's all I planned to see. There are pamphlets in the hotel that caught my interest. Did you know you can go to camps right out in the Barrens and watch the annual caribou migration? Thousands of them, with those gorgeous furry antlers. The desk clerk said it's quite a sight. Hunters go at this time of year, though. I wouldn't want to see that."

He didn't want her to see that, either, because in a couple of days his tour would start. The way things were going in town, it didn't matter how far the Barrens stretched—if she was there, too, they were bound to end up on the same patch of tundra. With the giver of the ring.

A few more days, she'd said. That would fit his calendar. By the time he got back to Yellow-knife, her holiday would be over. Life could return to normal.

WHEN SHE FIRST SAW THE Mountie looking like any other policeman, Sarah was disappointed.

"No red jacket?" she whispered to Ian. "No shiny leather boots? No riding crop?"

He was gorgeous, though. Sergeant Wainwright, of the Diamond Protection Service, was sandy haired, with a more or less military bearing and haircut, and a watchful manner that upped his charisma quotient. There was something about a watchful expression that always got to Sarah. It made her feel safe. Appreciated, too.

The sergeant, however, after one blue-eyed sweep for clues, was much too professional to appreciate her.

She did her best to play an efficient secretary, jotting notes in a booklet even though Ian had turned on a tape recorder.

The two men talked about security and organized crime, but Sarah's attention was mostly taken by the contrast between them. Dark hair versus blond. Casual fisherman of a freelancer versus perfectly uniformed officer. One trying to get a story, one trying not to give one. Wainwright wasn't only protecting diamonds, he was protecting information about diamonds.

When she and Ian were back out on the sidewalk, she said, "He wasn't very helpful, was he? That was a public relations report. He wanted to get a message out to crooks with an eye on his jurisdiction."

"Anyone who agrees to talk to a journalist has a message. In this case, that the RCMP is on the job."

Wainwright had listed ways criminals had tried to get a foot in the door. Drugs to hook mine workers, seduction and blackmail schemes, artificial diamonds or conflict diamonds smuggled in to sell as the real thing. All attempts defeated, he claimed.

The location of the mines helped, he'd told them, out in the middle of the tundra, close to the arctic circle. No roads until the ground and water froze; no towns for hundreds of miles; round-the-clock darkness in winter.

"It surprised me, how patient you were," Sarah said as they walked. "You didn't seem frustrated at all."

"I didn't expect to hear secrets."

"You know what's strange? Some of the people bustling around town probably aren't tourists or mining executives or geologists.

Some of them are probably drug-smuggling, blackmailing crooks."

It was a new idea for her, but Ian just smiled. He patted his camera, in a leather bag over his shoulder. "If only one of them would go into action."

"Oh! The photo-snapping crime fighter. I love it! And instead of being your secretary I'd be your sidekick. Do you have tights under your jeans?" She touched his belt. "Can I see?"

He gave her a look, reminding her that he, at least, was a grown-up.

Playing secretary was beginning to feel silly instead of fun. The feeling grew at the mining recorder's office. The interview didn't seem to be about diamonds at all. Only about the rules and laws of prospecting and mine development.

"No wonder you can be a bit grim," she said, when they left the office. "I had no idea journalism was like this. Where's the adventure?"

"This isn't where the dreams are, Sarah. It's only where the paperwork is done."

She could tell she had annoyed him. He was a man who appreciated rules. That had been one of the problems between them. Not during year one, their love affair, honeymoon, playing house year. During year two, responsibility had become his middle name. He'd wanted it to be hers, as well.

He'd drawn an invisible line dividing his idea of right from his idea of wrong, and, without meaning to, she'd continually crossed it. She would ask him for hints or a list of rules. He, ignoring the sarcasm, would claim there were no rules, only common sense.

She had oodles of common sense.

"The gem cutter's next," Ian said. "Mr. Jablonski. He's from Poland, an independent. He sells gems, cut or uncut, and finished jewelry, too. Maybe you can buy yourself a treat." He glanced at her hand, at engagement ring number three. "Or would that be redundant?"

"A diamond can't be redundant. It's a geological impossibility." She liked the idea of wearing one without a history, though, without promises and hopes attached.

But she wouldn't shop today. Her emotions had been getting a workout. She didn't want to think about promises or hopes, not broken ones and not brand-new shiny ones.

AT THE GEM CUTTER'S WORKSHOP they waited to be buzzed in, first at one door and then at a second. At the top of the stairs a man with a graying beard and very little hair stood behind a locked metal gate. He studied Ian's driver's license, then ushered them into his workroom and locked the door behind them.

Dim sunlight came through two small windows placed so high on the wall no one could see in or out. A fluorescent light dangled over a rectangular table, bare except for a piece of black felt.

Mr. Jablonski indicated a row of chairs on one side. "Sit, please." He got right to business. "You want to see rough?"

"If we may."

Shielding the locking mechanism from view, the man opened a safe and brought out a small drawstring bag. He sat across from Ian and Sarah, opened the bag and sprinkled a handful of uncut diamonds, translucent and gleaming rather than sparkling, onto the felt.

"Oh!" Sarah drew a deep breath and thought, *I want them.*

The man smiled. "Interested in buying?" With a pen, he separated one from the rest. "This I'd let you have for twenty thousand."

"I'll have to think about it."

After a quick smile, he separated a few more—smaller, but still larger than her ring. "These, eight thousand."

"Each? You're getting warmer. But no, thanks, I have enough."

"Enough diamonds?"

"Three. That's enough."

Was it really? Had she come to an unconscious decision—no more husbands? She couldn't imagine the next thirty years without at least one more try at wedded bliss.

"I have one that's similar to those." She held out her left hand.

"May I look closer?"

She took off her ring and passed it to him. He pulled a loupe from his pocket and studied the stone and its setting, making little sounds that seemed approving.

"A northern stone," Mr. Jablonski said. "See here?"

He showed Sarah where to look on the girdle of the diamond. She already knew about the etched symbol that promised the diamond was mined, cut and polished in the Northwest Territories, but she peered as directed.

"A very nice stone, beautifully cut," he told her. "Only a small inclusion."

"Jerod said it was perfect."

"Next to perfect, I assure you. When is the happy day?"

The news of the inclusion had distracted her,

so it took her a second to answer. "Been and gone, I'm afraid. No need to throw out the baby with the bath water, though, right?"

Ian had been snapping pictures of the rough. He stopped and stared at her, his expression as focused as the gem cutter's had been while looking through the loupe. As watchful as Wainwright's had been, talking about criminals. Had she crossed another of his invisible lines?

He turned to Mr. Jablonski. "I'll admit to being puzzled about the lure of diamonds. To me they don't look that different from quartz or cut glass."

"Mr. Kingsley, you must not have seen a perfect stone. Even this one—" The gem cutter indicated Sarah's hand.

Even this one?

"—reflects and holds the light in a way glass or quartz never could. It's clear and sparkling— like the arctic ice, yes?" He touched his chest. "When I see these northern stones, so beautiful, so pure, my heart goes quiet."

His genuine emotion moved Sarah. This was more the way she had imagined a story about diamonds would be. It made up for the disappointing visit to the mining recorder's office.

Mr. Jablonski showed them more stones and

finally some finished jewelry. Sarah wanted every piece she saw. If she saved forever, she'd be lucky to afford even one. It was really uncomfortable to get a glimpse of the kind of temptation a thief might feel.

The interview complete, they went back through the locked gate and the two locked doors into bright sunshine.

Sarah held her hand to the light and tilted it this way and that. The stone sparkled. There was no sign of a flaw.

"Have you hypnotized yourself?"

She moved her hand so Ian got full benefit of the stone's light-refracting powers. "Do you really not feel it?"

"Avarice?"

"Awe."

"Neither."

For someone who put so much stock in seeing things for what they were, he went out of his way to deny the value and appeal of diamonds. Did it bother him to see her wearing another man's ring? No need to tell him his was around her neck.

"Did you hear him? *Even* this one, he said. And I wore it especially for him, too!"

"You wore the ring for Mr. Jablonski?"

They had started walking back to her hotel.

Sarah didn't want the afternoon to end. "Why don't we stop for a late lunch or an early dinner?"

"Sorry. I need to go through the tapes while the interviews are fresh in my memory."

"Later, then?"

Honestly. Her own tongue was her worst enemy.

"Later there's a thing—"

"A thing?"

"Just a casual get-together." He sounded uncomfortable. "Local press and whoever else shows up."

"And you were going without me?" She meant to say it teasingly, but she was afraid it sounded indignant. Needy.

"Did you…want to go?"

She heard his reluctance. "I'd love to. What time should I be ready?"

He didn't answer immediately. She could back off, say she'd changed her mind.

"Pick you up at eight?"

"Perfect."

CHAPTER NINE

SARAH HAD CHANGED INTO jeans that hugged her body and a red top, the silky one from the other night, really striking with her dark hair and pale skin. Her shoes were nothing but straps and a little heel. Why did she think they were a good choice for walking to the Old Town? She still wore the large, almost perfect diamond that apparently didn't have to signal an engagement.

He liked the way she smelled. It wasn't a perfume; she found those overpowering. When he first knew her, at least, she'd used scented lotions and soaps. He'd nuzzle in, sniffing loudly to make her laugh, trying to guess if it was lavender or cloves or pear….

Ian straightened, certain his nose had pulled him into a diagonal line pointing at the back of her neck.

"Truce for the evening, right?" Sarah said. "We'll relax? No analysis of motives, no accusations."

"Truce," he agreed. "What you said earlier… behave ourselves. Sit in chairs. Talk the way people do."

"Otherwise known as fun."

"I'm all about fun." He said it straight-faced.

When they reached the harbor she sat on a bench overlooking the water, and patted the spot beside her. "Sit with me awhile. It's so beautiful here. Let's enjoy it. Doesn't it remind you of my family's cottage?"

It did. He'd gone there with her a few times—canoed and swam, picked blueberries and made love under the stars. Even though the cottage was so much farther south, in the Whiteshell, near the borders with Minnesota and Ontario, it was the same kind of terrain. "It's all Precambrian Shield."

"Wild, but idyllic. I could live here."

Ian snorted. Sarah couldn't live anywhere but a big city that offered constant and varied entertainment.

"I absolutely could!"

"You'd go nuts in two weeks."

"Because?"

Lattes came to mind, but of course she could get lattes in Yellowknife. She'd miss boutiques that sold Italian silk clothes, though, or whatever that red fabric was that sort of rippled over her body.

Ian tried to push the thought out of his mind, but once he'd pictured the rippling, the image froze, like on a crashed computer screen. No matter how many times a person clicked on the little X in the corner of the screen, frozen pictures didn't go away.

Well, unless he rebooted.

There was an idea. Clear the screen, clear the memory.

Trouble was, he didn't want to do it. He wanted her on the screen. He wanted his memories.

"You wouldn't like the winters," he told her.

"Maybe not the all-day nights and the forty below, but I'd certainly like the light show."

Oh, she would. When she'd seen the northern lights in the south, dim and white and hardly moving, she'd gasped, hands to her chest, so moved he'd watched her and not them. Here, at the right time of year, they filled the sky. They swirled and crackled like flames, like billowing curtains, and they morphed to shades of green, red, violet. If she saw those, she'd rhapsodize over them, and then she'd cry.

"Ready to go?"

She let him pull her to her feet and then kept

holding his hand until, under the pretext of slapping a mosquito, he got it free.

THE PARTY WAS IN full swing. A broad-shouldered man of about thirty-five came toward them, grinning. Resting one heavy arm on Ian's shoulders, he smiled at Sarah.

"Where did you find this bit of loveliness?"

While Sarah wondered whether or not she minded a complete stranger talking about her that way, Ian answered in a friendly yet warning tone, "English Lit, twelve long years ago."

"No kidding? Old friends, are you?" The man held out a large hand, which Sarah hesitated to take. She risked it, and got the life squeezed out of her fingers, as expected.

"Mike Tremblay. Outfitter to the stars." He winked at Ian as he asked Sarah, "Are we going to be lucky enough to have you along for the ride?"

"No," Ian said.

"What ride?" Sarah asked.

"Five days' exploration of the Territories. Your friend has wisely seen he can't catch the flavor of this huge land by staying in town. Wonderful city, don't get me wrong, but he's looking in the window here. Granted, he's taking a good, long look, but it's still from outside."

"And you're going to take him inside?"

"Not all the way. He doesn't have time for that, but we'll do the best we can. Let me show you something." He led her to a window overlooking a series of docks, most of them with small airplanes tied to them. "See there? That's the floatplane base. And that's my little darlin'."

Sarah couldn't see which plane he meant, but they all looked alarmingly delicate. "What's it like to fly in one of those?"

"Exhilarating!"

Her stomach lurched at the word.

"We're going to see falls that are twice as long as the ones at Niagara. We're going to visit a diamond exploration camp and help search for indicator minerals."

"Indicator?"

"Those are other gems in diamond-bearing rock. Garnets, mostly. There are a lot more of them than there are diamonds, so you're more likely to find them. And if you do, it's time to drill."

"You drill for diamonds?" Sarah asked.

"You drill for a sample of kimberlite—" He broke off. "You'll understand once you get there and see for yourself."

"I'd love to go."

Ian had followed them to the window. "You really wouldn't, Sarah."

"We'll likely see the caribou herd," Mike added, "all kinds of birds and we'll even dip our toes in the Arctic Ocean. I want Ian—and his readers—to get the whole picture."

"Count me in, Mike. I want to get the whole picture, too."

While the outfitter exclaimed how great it would be to have her along, Ian hurried to tell her how much she'd hate it. Bugs and outdoor biffies topped his list. Sarah had to admit to a dislike of both, but the thought of tundra, of actually crossing the arctic circle, was more powerful. It seemed almost mythical, a journey Liz absolutely needed to take.

"You don't have much time to prepare," Mike said. "Go to Weaver and Devore tomorrow, they'll set you up." He mangled her hand again, pounded Ian's shoulder and went off into the crowd.

"It wouldn't be fun for you, Sarah," Ian said. "There'd be nothing for you to do. No restaurants. No stores. I'll be working nonstop."

"I know. I'll help." She made a face, mocking herself. "Like I did today." He could come right out and tell her she wasn't welcome on his trip, but he wasn't doing that, he was only dissuading. Not effectively, either. So maybe he didn't really mind if she went, too.

The old man she'd met at the lake had come to the party. He sat with a fragile, white-haired woman dressed in clothes as worn as his.

Sarah pulled Ian's arm to get his attention. "Do you see that couple? At the table under the antlers? I met him yesterday morning and embarrassed myself by offering him money. He looked in need, but he wouldn't take it."

"Danny Ferguson," Ian said. "He won't take money unless you have a drink with him, Sarah. Then it's companionship, not charity."

"He accepted your money, did he?"

"We shared a few pints last week. He came from Newfoundland in the fifties to work on the DEW line, met the love of his life and stayed. Her parents had better things in mind for her, an education, a career, but once she'd met Danny she didn't want anything else."

"So they've had fifty years together."

"More."

Half a century with one person. How many mornings was that? How many arguments, how many cups of tea? "He told you a lot about himself. I remember you being a good listener. Sometimes."

"It's my job. A place plus a person equals a story."

"That's poetic."

"That's journalism." The word poetic had brought his guard back up. "Can I get you a drink?"

"Is there anything local?"

"An Alberta beer, I think. Close enough? I'll check."

No sooner had Ian gone, winding his way toward the bar, then a six-foot-two linebacker type detached himself from the group he was with and headed straight for Sarah. He lurched in front of her, staring with alcohol-fueled intensity. All he was missing was a sign that read This Is the Guy Ian Warned You to Avoid.

"I'm gonna buy you dinner."

She tried not to breathe in the fumes. "Thanks, but I've eaten."

He thought about that, then devised a new plan. "I'm gonna take you for a walk." She backed away when he lifted a hand to touch her hair. "You and me, the sun goin' down…"

She saw Ian returning, without their drinks, walking quickly. He extended an arm to make a sort of corridor for her and began guiding her away.

"Hey." The man shoved him.

"Oh, be careful!" Sarah said, but there was no need to worry about Ian. He held the man still, one arm twisted behind his back.

"Ready to go back to your friends?" Ian's voice was calm.

The man nodded.

"And you'll leave this lady alone."

He nodded again.

Ian released him, and he tottered away.

Sarah had dealt with unwanted attention before and in a room full of people she was sure she would have been fine. She was touched, though, that Ian had hurried to help her.

"You rescued me."

"Or embarrassed you. You could have handled him."

"Rescued," she said firmly. She put one hand on his chest, a thank-you touch, but left it there because the warmth of his skin through the fabric felt good. "Doesn't that mean my life belongs to you?"

He stood stiffly, his expression neutral. Not drawing her in. Not pushing her away. "Only this next ten or fifteen minutes, till you're safe at your hotel."

"I'm not going to my hotel."

"After that demonstration? Five times as many men as women are crowding this place, and a lot of them are looking for a good time. You plan to stay here, all tantalizing?"

She raised her eyebrows at the word. "I wasn't trying to be tantalizing."

"I know you weren't."

She moved closer, running her hand from his chest down his side to his waist. She was only playing but the longer the game went on, the harder that was to remember. "Are you saying it just happened, that I couldn't help myself? I'm a force of nature?"

He looked as if he really wished he could take back the last few minutes.

"You're saying I can't help tantalizing men any more than the wind can help blowing?"

Ian gave in. "And men can't help being tantalized anymore than a tree can help being blown over."

"Yet here you stand so sturdily."

"Darn right."

"Nothing wrong with swaying a little."

"Already did that."

"And you're never, ever going to sway again?"

"Sarah…"

"Stop?"

"It isn't that. But we're done, right? Long done."

She nodded. Ten years done. Did he think she was chasing him? It must seem that way. She certainly wasn't. She'd never chased a man in her life. But there was something about him she couldn't leave alone. He was the same as he used to be in many ways, but so different, too. The mystery of the differences grabbed her. The mystery of the ten years apart.

She let go of his shirt. "It's fun seeing you again."

"It's fun seeing you, too."

She smiled. "Is it?"

"It's having its moments."

That seemed like a huge step forward. Even if he was only being agreeable because they'd called a truce, it was still progress. She didn't ask herself progress toward what. She just let herself feel happy.

"So we'll have an adventure. Explore the North together, work on your article—I'll be your Girl Friday!"

"Sarah Bretton volunteering to make the coffee? I don't believe it."

"No, no, no. But everywhere you go, I'll go, with a sharp pencil and a booklet. I'll take notes."

"That's what my tape recorder's for."

"And whenever you make a mistake I'll let you know. I'll edit you."

"Thanks a bunch."

"I'm a good editor."

"I'm sure you are. But I'm famous for not needing one."

"Everyone needs an editor."

"Think back, Sarah. All those classes we had together. Did I ever make a spelling, punctuation or grammar mistake?"

She looked into space, eyes narrowed in thought.

"Well?"

"Searching, searching…"

"You know I didn't."

"Then I'll be your fact-checker. You must need one of those."

"It wouldn't hurt." He seemed sorry to admit it.

Sarah flung her arms out from her sides in a voilà gesture. "Then we have a deal, an honest-to-goodness working relationship." Her arms were at the ready; wrapping them around him was only natural. So was standing on her toes, so was touching her lips to his…

"Hey," he said. "Kissing the boss is never a good idea."

"Boss? Sweetie pie, we're partners."

CHAPTER TEN

The next morning Sarah went to Weaver and Devore to stock up on camping supplies. When she returned to the hotel she stopped at the front desk and arranged to keep her room and Liz's while they were away.

She'd already told her parents she wouldn't be visiting, after all. They'd understood the time pressures connected to Liz's book, but she still felt guilty. A couple of years earlier her father had almost had a heart attack—a warning, his doctor had said. Since then she'd done her best not to raise his blood pressure but no matter how hard she tried, she was more likely to add stress to his life than lessen it. There'd been worry and disappointment in his voice even as he wished her an exciting and productive trip.

Now she had to let Oliver know she would be away from the office longer than planned.

"It's all right with me," he said, when Sarah

called to explain. "I'll warn you, though. Jenny and I have bonded over the past few days. Another week, and separating us might not be the right thing to do. This morning I showed her your picture and she simply didn't care."

Sarah laughed, but not without regret. She was afraid it was true. "I'll bring her a Northwest Territories souvenir. You, too."

"Will it be bigger than a bread box?"

"Smaller."

"A diamond?"

"Bigger. There's a chance, Oliver, I'll bring you something that says, 'by Elizabeth Robb.'"

"Be still my heart! Off you go, then. I'll explain to the pup."

While she was trying on her new bug jacket and bug hat, Ian dropped by. He said he wanted to discuss the trip's ground rules but he didn't seem to have them ready.

"It's a work trip," she prompted, trying to help him get started.

"Right."

"No heels."

He smiled faintly. "That would be advisable."

She removed her bug hat, the better to see while she rummaged through bags on the bed. "I bought a pair of waterproof, bug-proof, slip-proof shoes you're really going to love." They didn't quickly come to hand, so she gave up looking. "They're the highest-tech pair of shoes I've ever seen. All they're missing is a clock alarm and an espresso maker."

"You didn't get the top of the line, then."

Smiling, Sarah moved on to the next item that must be on his list. "You won't have time to rescue me from drunken louts."

"Louts, yes. But not bugs. Or bitter coffee."

"You think I can't take care of myself on a camping trip? Don't you worry. The Brettons are tough! We hike and climb, canoe, cook over fires. Remember summers at the lake?"

"I remember wicker chairs on the porch and roasted marshmallows. Stacks of mystery novels."

"You, sir, have a faulty memory. We'll see soon enough. I'm almost ready. Got my gear, called Oliver—he's my partner at Fraser Press, remember?—he's agreed to look after Jenny for another week."

"Jenny?"

"My dog. She's the sweetest thing. I found her in an animal shelter. Our eyes locked and that was it."

Ian looked at the piles of supplies on the bed, the sofa and the desk. "Have you spent every penny you had?"

"There'll be more. Every couple of weeks a bunch of pennies lands in my account." She made a fluttering motion with the fingers of one hand, indicating the money's journey. He looked annoyed, so she did it again.

"Two jackets? Two sleeping bags?"

"My friend Liz is coming."

"Your friend Liz is coming on my trip north?"

"Our trip."

"My trip, Sarah."

"Ian, don't be annoyed. Mike invited me. I'm helping you."

"And now your friend Liz, whoever she may be, is going to help me, too?"

"No, I'm helping her."

"Wonderful. You've set up some kind of aid organization—"

"She has to come, Ian. She's arriving tomorrow to visit. I can't take off the next day."

"I have a deadline."

"So does she. Only it's past already. She's my main author. The one who's stuck. The big, money-draining problem."

He laughed. "Oh, Lord. It's going to be a regular writers' retreat up there." He pointed a finger at her. "Nothing touchy-feely, Sarah. No emotional exercises. I'm not getting in touch with anything."

"Horrible, horrible touchy-feeliness, absolutely not."

"Have you talked to Mike? I don't know if the plane will take another passenger and her gear."

"Just one little extra person."

Ian stared at her hard. "You haven't asked him, have you? Didn't you think of it? Out of courtesy, even? Forget safety codes, how about to be polite?"

Sarah opened her mouth to protest, but was stopped by an unwelcome burst of insight. She had been rude, inconsiderate, thoughtless—all the things her brothers had accused her of being since she was old enough to crawl after them.

"I'll ask him now."

Ian was leaving.

"I should have asked him before," she conceded, raising her voice as the door shut. "But I'll ask now."

THE NEXT EVENING SARAH watched the 737 that carried Liz descend, growing bigger until she could clearly see the Northwest Territories emblem on its tail wing. With a roar of engines it touched down and taxied to the terminal. Ten minutes later Liz appeared from around the polar bear display that dominated the arrivals area.

She looked exhausted. From Three Creeks to Winnipeg to Edmonton to Yellowknife, including all the time needed to check in and get past security, must have taken eight or ten hours. Sarah wasn't sure how she'd break the news that more air time had been worked into their schedule. Bright and early tomorrow, they'd be getting back on a plane. A bush plane.

Liz hadn't lost all her baby weight. She'd never been skinny, so now she had a definite rounded appearance. She seemed to be trying to hide it under a baggy shirt that hung over her bottom and beyond. Except for the lack of color splotches, it could have been a painting smock.

An urge to wrap her wayward author in blankets and begin enticing her with chocolate and tea was stymied when Liz held up a finger to indicate she needed a minute, and headed for a pay phone.

"Sweetheart?" Sarah heard her say, after a moment. "I'm here safely. How's Rose?" Liz listened for a long time, smiling fondly and then giving directions about applesauce.

"Did you get the trees in?" Domestic details followed, how many spruce trees had been planted, and how many fir, and where the muscle rub was kept, and to remember it was a medicine and to not use more of it than the package said.

Finally Sarah heard kisses, suction-cup loud ones for the baby. From all the murmured you, too's and me, too's, she thought she caught the gist of what passed between Liz and Jack. She began to feel like an evil witch who had torn apart honeymooners. But Liz and Jack weren't honeymooners. They'd been together for something like five years. An old married couple.

At last Liz hung up.

"Everyone all right?" Sarah asked.

"So far, so good. This is the longest I've ever been away."

Ten hours? "Since the baby, you mean?"

"I went out for lunch with my cousin once, but it was during nap time. I hope Jack and Rose will be okay for a few days."

"Of course they will."

"Rose won't understand why I'm not there. And if the weather's good, Jack can't stay with her. He has to get the trees in."

"Good thing you live in Robbtown."

Liz smiled weakly. "Rose knows them all."

"She won't even miss you." From the look on Liz's face, Sarah guessed that wasn't quite the right thing to say. She added, "Not enough to stay awake nights, I mean. Or lose her appetite. She'll cope."

Liz still didn't look very impressed with her.

Really, she should have stayed away from empty reassurances. What did she know about mothers and babies? She tried again. "It must be hard to leave her."

Liz's eyes filled with tears. She raised her hands to her face, using her fingers to hold back a flood. "Oh, dear. I'm sorry."

"Hormones," Sarah said sympathetically.

Liz shot her an aggravated look. "You see a tear and the first thing that comes to your mind is hormones? You're as bad as a man, Sarah."

Worse. Oliver would never mention an author's hormones. Sarah decided to stop trying to find the perfect, healing phrase, and instead shepherd this poor shell of Elizabeth Robb to the hotel.

A COOL BREEZE BROUGHT faint music, voices and traffic sounds through the open balcony door into Sarah's room. Liz had admired the views of the lake and the red-tinged tundra beyond the city, but seemed too tired to really take it in. She sat in the hotel's deep, uphol-stered club chair, her feet raised on the matching ottoman.

Sarah had made tea. She poured two cups and handed one to Liz.

"Should we talk about the manuscript?"

"I don't think so."

It wasn't as if Sarah had expected the flight itself, or the comforts of the hotel room, to cure Liz. The sights and sounds of the Barrens would do that. The word alone—Barrens— made Sarah want to write, and she wasn't even a writer. Someone like Liz would be beside herself.

They'd been working together for eight years and, maybe because of similar backgrounds, they had become something like friends. Both had grown up in Manitoba and had rushed into early marriages, Sarah during first year university and Liz right after high school. Within weeks Liz's eighteen-year-old husband had died, and she, blaming her friends and her community for an accident that should never have happened, had moved away. Stayed away for fifteen years. That was a long time to hold on to anger. Some things couldn't be forgiven.

Liz must have managed it, though, because she'd gone back. Found love again. Three Creeks hadn't stopped her writing. Marriage hadn't. But for now, at least, motherhood had.

"So," Sarah said. "The book."

Liz closed her eyes.

"I wish I didn't have to press, but we have so little time." She paused, but Liz didn't comment. Sarah prompted, "You weren't happy with your story idea."

"All my stories are more or less the same, aren't they? Plucky child, big adventure."

"They're not the same. Plucky fairies, big battles. Real boy, real nature. Time travel, castles." That one had come after Liz and Jack's honeymoon in England.

"Plucky children time travel to castles."

"I won't let you dismiss your work, Liz. Children love your books. That's always made you happy. Very happy."

"Maybe I'm just tired."

"And that's why nobody's going to demand your attention as long as you're here. Nobody's going to wake you up at night."

"Lovely."

Sarah hated to follow those assurances with what she now realized was a demand for Liz's attention, but there wasn't time to put off her announcement. "I've been a bad friend."

"To?"

"You."

"Don't tell me, let me guess. You can't stand another moment in the same territory as your ex and you're going back to Vancouver tonight?"

In the taxi Liz had displayed that unwavering need for detailed explanations that seemed peculiar to teachers and parents. So she knew about the column and the impulse to visit Ian.

"I wouldn't do that to you."

"Good. So what did you do to me?"

"I've arranged to go north with him."

"With Ian? Haven't we already gone north?"

"More north. Into the Barren Lands. Don't you love the sound of that?"

"I'm not sure."

"I was hoping you'd like to go, too." Sarah thought of the stack of camping equipment she'd bought. Hoping was an understatement. Counting on would be closer to the truth.

"Barren Lands," Liz repeated, stressing both words.

"Doesn't that draw you in? Doesn't it say adventure?"

"Oh, I see. Plucky Sarah and Liz."

"There'll be no need for pluck."

"Don't the mosquitoes weigh five pounds up there?"

"No more than three, I promise. We'd go in a bush plane, Liz. Bush planes opened up the North. How can any self-respecting writer not seize that chance? We're going to camp with a diamond prospector. See polar bears."

Sarah wasn't sure the last part was true and,

really, she hoped they wouldn't see any. Polar bears were cute in cartoons, but big, fast and ferocious in real life. "They should be slow in the summer, though, I'll bet," she said out loud. "Because they're so desperately underfed when the ice retreats."

"Slow, desperate, hungry. Which of those conditions do you think would influence their behavior most?"

"Liz, you wouldn't have to worry about a thing. The arrangements are all taken care of. I bought two of everything, sleeping bags, jackets, bear spray—"

"Stop right there. Tell me you said hair spray."

"Sorry."

Liz's voice became firm. "Sarah, I thought you were joking about polar bears."

"I know," she said soothingly. "I agree completely. And normally I require more than a piece of waterproof fabric between me and a bear. But I really need to do this." She corrected herself. "We need to do this."

"Go north with Ian Kingsley."

"Not *with* him. Just…concurrently." Sarah hesitated. Liz was looking at her in a way that made her very uncomfortable. "Did you know you've already learned how to do that maternal expression? The glare. The one that says you see right through me and my lies."

"I do see right through you and your lies. And I don't like camping."

"Me, neither. But there'll be tundra. There'll be ptarmigan and lemmings."

"And yet you didn't buy lemming spray."

"Did you bring paints?"

Liz hadn't. Sarah ran to the closet, found the right bag and with a flourish, handed it to Liz, who lifted one edge to peek inside.

"Oh, Sarah." She pulled out a sketch book, a watercolor pad, a set of charcoal pencils and a rectangular wooden box full of tubes of paint.

"Because you're going to be inspired, you know you are," Sarah said happily. "In another bag you'll find a collapsible easel. It's going to be a wonderful trip, Liz. You're going to love it."

"I already miss Jack and Rose."

"That will make it even better when you see them again." Sarah led Liz back to the chair. "Sit down, put your feet up. I'll pour another cup of tea. Would you like chocolate? We have raspberry truffles."

"You're pampering me."

"Of course. Two hours of pampering, a good night's sleep, then we meet the cold, hard North."

"All of a sudden it's cold and hard? What happened to fun and inspiring?"

"I'm just saying, enjoy the two hours."

CHAPTER ELEVEN

THE OTTER BANKED, sending Sarah's just-eaten breakfast sideways and showing off the peaks and canyons of the Mackenzie Mountains. Mike had taken them to the southwest corner of the Northwest Territories, over Nahanni National Park. Sarah's brain told her the scenery was beyond beautiful, it was glorious, but her stomach didn't care.

When the plane had started banging across the wide-open waters of Great Slave Lake, pontoons hitting each wave like a sledgehammer on rock, she'd realized she'd made a terrible mistake. As challenging as she found airliners to be, floatplanes were an entirely different species.

Ian sat in the front, beside Mike. Since takeoff, his camera had been attached to his face, Borglike, but each time the plane stood on a wing tip, the better to show them wood bison grazing below, he'd turned to smile encouragingly. He knew. Despite his many flaws, the man could be a sweetheart. Maybe if they'd lived in an airplane things would have worked out better....

Mike tilted the plane and stabbed his finger at the window. "Virginia Falls!"

A mass of moving water. White, roiling, cascading over and down gray crags of rock to a turquoise pool far below. In crannies nearby Sarah saw goats or sheep, whichever they were, the big, shaggy, curly-horned ones.

"Amazing!" Liz shouted in Sarah's ear. "I wish Jack was here to see this!"

Sarah managed a tight-lipped smile. This was what she'd hoped for, an adventure to stimulate Liz.

The plane began to drop, following the line of the mountain. At closer range Sarah saw that her turquoise pool was something less peaceful, churning foam where the falls hit the water.

Again, Mike jabbed at the ground. "Nahanni River! Nahanni, that's Deh Cho for spirit." Flying low, he followed the river until the rapids calmed. The Nahanni meandered through green, wooded hills, finally joining another river that flowed north.

"This is the Laird!" Mike shouted.

He took the plane lower, level with the

treetops, heading across the river toward a small island. The pontoons made contact and they bounced along like a huge skipping stone, slowing at last and coasting in to dock.

Mike turned, grinning. "Well, ladies?"

"Amazing," Liz said again. Limited vocabulary, Sarah thought sourly, considering she made a living as a writer, but at least she sounded interested in the world outside Three Creeks.

Sarah didn't do much better herself. "Big mountain." An overly simple observation, but all she could manage, unless she added *big water* or *big tummy ache*. Or *please, please, please take me home. By car.*

"'Bout nine thousand feet," Mike agreed, and obligingly provided more stats—acres, peaks, explorers—while Sarah wobbled out of the plane.

Ian helped her down. "Better now?"

She stood close to him, absorbing comfort from his body. Warmth and strength flowed out of him, into her. He was like that sometimes, calm in the face of a storm.

"Is this one of the towns without roads, Ian?" So many northern communities could only be reached by air or water except in the coldest months, when the frozen ground allowed for sled dogs or snowmobiles and, in some spots, ice roads.

"There's a road, but it's the last one we'll be near for a while. If you want to make a run for it, you'd better do it now."

She let go of his hand. Unless she had imagined it, his voice had cooled. She remembered she'd told him Brettons were tough. She'd promised she wouldn't need looking after.

"I'm where I jumped, right?"

"Where you insisted on jumping."

The mood had changed very quickly. It must have been obvious to the others because Mike spoke extra loud and a little too heartily. "This, ladies and gentleman, is the town of Fort Simpson. Why are we here? I'm glad you asked."

Sarah and Ian moved farther apart, letting Mike guide them away from the river while he told them about the town.

"There's a pay phone," Liz said, her voice lifting happily. She hurried off, digging in her pockets for change and saying over her shoulder that they should go ahead, she'd catch up later.

She did so much later, after they'd stopped at a store to pick up antidotes for headaches and nausea, eaten lunch and begun to explore the island on which Fort Simpson stood. All Liz had on her mind was news from home. Rose was doing fine without her, which was a huge relief to her, but also a bit of a shock.

Ian and Mike had walked along the shore, stooping to examine things underfoot, gesturing to the mountains beyond and to some kind of bird flying high above. Ian, as far as Sarah could tell, was in his element.

"I married a frontier man," she said, only half believing it. "You know that Robert Redford character, the one who hunted and trapped and lived in the mountains? That's who I married."

"Lucky you. Except then you unmarried him."

"Well, you know, those mountain men don't go in for a lot of washing and shaving. Talking, either."

"How much talking does a girl need?"

Liz's voice had deepened suggestively, out of keeping with the way Sarah saw her, a children's author, the mother of a baby. "I need a lot of talking."

Laughing, Liz walked faster, toward Mike and Ian.

Sarah called after her, "A lot of intelligent, thoughtful talking. What's funny about that? A lot of washing, too. And a lot of shaving."

Liz waved without turning around. Sarah

watched her join the men, who were now admiring the spot where the quiet Laird River met the wide MacKenzie.

POOR SARAH, IAN THOUGHT. She'd been green around the gills the whole time they'd been on the ground, had skipped the caribou burgers offered for lunch, and when they'd headed back to the Otter, she'd gone with the pale resignation of an aristocrat to the guillotine.

She'd never been much for air travel. When her parents had given them a trip to Vancouver Island as a wedding gift she'd clung to him the whole way, tighter with every air pocket and every ding of the seat belt or washroom door bell. Food had been out of the question then, too. He'd turned down his own meal rather than risk upsetting her more. He'd felt like her protector. A brand-new feeling for a nineteen-year-old.

Nineteen. Had anyone tried to stop them, reason with them? Vaguely he remembered his parents' dismay when he'd called with the news. After all those years saving to help him with his tuition they must have been fairly sure he'd collect a degree before a wife. Their reaction had been restrained, though. Why not wait until after graduation? they'd asked. Sarah's parents, looking for the least of two evils, had suggested he and their only daughter just move in together.

At lunch Mike had told them more about their next stop, a diamond exploration camp where they'd spend a couple of days and nights. It wasn't just any camp. It belonged to his fiancée, a Dene geologist. She spent every summer out in the Barrens while he operated his one-plane outfitter's company. One day, he'd said, it would be solidly on its feet and she'd have found her diamonds. Then, at last, they could marry and live under the same roof twelve months of the year.

"Down there," Mike called. "One of the diamond mines."

Ian noticed even Sarah perked up at that news. The antinausea meds must have kicked in. There wasn't anything sparkly for her to see from this distance. Rolling tundra, lakes and, like a colony on the moon, rows of white, rectangular buildings. The main feature was a round, gaping hole—an open pit mine terraced out of the rock, going hundreds of feet into the ground. It reminded him of a Roman amphitheater.

"Can you go in low?"

"They don't like that. Security." Mike grinned, then began a descent. "Tell me when."

The Otter went lower, then lower still, until

hard-hatted, orange-vested figures looked up, their consternation obvious.

"When," Ian called.

They passed over the site once. He took several wide-angle shots, getting an overview of the mine in its setting. Then he circled a finger in the air and Mike banked to do another pass. This time Ian zoomed in on trucks full of ore reaching the surface. A great shot for his next column, side by side with one from Jablon-ski's workshop. Tons of ore, tiny pile of diamonds.

He gave Mike a thumbs-up and the plane pulled away, gaining altitude again.

Mike asked, "Want to take it for a spin?"

"The Otter? You kidding? Sure."

"Keep her straight and level." He pointed ahead. "Follow the river till it empties into a small lake. Then I'll show you how to bank to the west."

Ian nodded, without mentioning he'd flown before. Because of all the lakes and muskeg in northern Manitoba, roads had never been built going in and out of Churchill. Bush planes were a common form of travel, so learning to fly had come naturally.

Mike's plane was a bit of a senior citizen, an original Otter, but it handled beautifully. Ian kept his hands light on the wheel, correcting the rudder peddle from time to time. His camera and his story ebbed from his mind. So did his mixed and confusing feelings about Sarah. He floated, unencumbered, light as air.

WHEN MIKE'S HANDS LEFT the wheel, like an idiot, daredevil kid on a bike, Sarah was sure the plane would turn nose down and drop straight to the ground.

But Ian seemed to know what to do. He checked dials and arrows on the instrument panel and pressed or switched knobs. No emergency signals went off. When he looked over at Mike, he grinned in a carefree way she'd never seen before. *This is the life,* his body said.

She tried to ignore that Mike wasn't in control of the plane, then tried to ignore that she was in a plane at all. That didn't go very well, because Liz kept drawing her attention to things like wisps of cloud touching the wing tips. Whenever the plane shuddered or got caught, kitelike, on the wind, Liz grinned and said some variation of how much Jack would like this.

Sarah tensed at a change in the engine sound. The plane turned and began to go lower. Instinctively, she reached for something to grasp, and found Liz's hand. Ian was still flying the plane. Mike wasn't going to let him land it, was he?

She chanced a look out the window. More of that latticework of rock and water, and tufts of that reddish plant she'd seen from the hotel. Straggly trees grew by a small lake. Half-hidden in those were a few white tents.

Ian flew over the lake, circled and came in lower. The flaps on the wings went down. He pulled back on the wheel and gently, gently, the plane touched the water. Sarah breathed for what felt like the first time in an hour, then noticed she was still clutching Liz's hand.

"Sorry! Did I bruise your fingers?"

"I'll never hold a paintbrush again, but that's all right." Liz leaned over the seat to talk to Mike. "Have we crossed the arctic circle?"

"Not yet." He winked. "Two more sleeps."

"It's still summer here. I thought we'd outrun it."

"You'd have to go a long way to do that. Even when we reach Tuktoyaktuk, right on the ocean, it'll be summer. Chilly summer, mind you."

A dark haired woman emerged from one of the tents and came to the lake to meet them.

"Marie, darlin'!"

"Mike." With that one word, she expressed

disapproval, question and warning. She was pretty and petite, not Sarah's idea of a geologist. "You didn't mention passengers."

"Don't I get a kiss?"

Wasn't he picking up the freezing vibes? Sarah wondered. Or did he hope to smile his way through them? It wouldn't work. If there'd been an opportunity to advise him she would have told him to tread softly.

"I brought you some company." He began the introductions. The award-winning journalist, the famous children's author and—here he made the added mistake of putting a hand on Sarah's back and leaving it there—the author's editor.

When he referred to her as the lovely Sarah Bretton, she began to think he meant to be provocative.

"Sarah's a real city slicker," he said, with apparent affection, "but she's going to tough it out with us for the next couple of days."

"Good for Sarah," Marie said acidly.

"Sarah loves diamonds," Mike added.

"I'm sure she does."

"So I thought she'd get a kick out of helping you look for them."

Sarah decided it was past time to change the focus of the conversation. "I'm very happy to meet you, Marie. I'm afraid we might be intruding." She pointed first to Ian, then to Liz. "I'm here to fact-check for him and to give aid and comfort to her. Mike flies, Ian researches and hopefully Liz gets inspired. I'm sort of the bump on the log."

Marie smiled faintly and looked slightly less angry.

Ian pitched in. "The trip's all my fault. I wanted to see what a diamond hunt is like."

"The first thing it's like," Marie said, "is confidential."

An uncomfortable silence followed.

No one else had come out of the tents to greet the plane and Sarah didn't see anyone working in the surrounding area. "Are you here alone?"

"At the moment, yes." Marie gave Mike a less unfriendly look than the ones he'd got so far. "He stays for a few days sometimes. My brothers come, or kids from my village, to learn the ropes. What I've got here for now is a cottage industry. Without proof of a diamond-bearing pipe, investors are hard to find."

"Pipe?" Sarah asked.

"A wedge of kimberlite. That's the kind of stone that carries diamonds."

"I thought rivers carried diamonds."

"They can. They're not the source."

Every answer led to more questions, but Marie didn't seem to be in the mood for discussion. Sarah decided to wait.

After Ian showed Marie his first column and explained that this week he was focusing on the diamond industry, she began—still reluctantly, Sarah thought—to make the best of it. She gave them a quick tour of the camp, telling them the basic safety rules about propane use, wood fires and food storage as they went.

She was using traditional white canvas prospector's tents, tall enough to stand in, with wooden floors, and stoves that vented to the outside. There were four of them. One for sleeping and another for working stood within a few yards of each other. Some distance away was a cook tent, and lastly, even farther away, one that housed the latrine. An electric fence, with bells attached as an added precaution, surrounded the camp.

The diamond exploration area stretched far beyond the protective wire. Marie told them animals had never bothered her while she hiked or dug and sifted the dirt. She'd seen caribou and the odd wolf, but had always been treated as part of the landscape. As far as predators went, the important thing was not to give them cause to associate humans with food. To be on the safe side she usually carried a shotgun when she went outside the fence.

She looked at Sarah, and there was no mistaking the challenge in her expression. "Anyone want to go out with me?"

Sarah didn't let herself hesitate. "I'd love to go. But if I find any diamonds they're mine, right?" She smiled to show she was joking, but she could see Marie didn't think it was funny. Not at all.

IAN DIDN'T BLAME MARIE for being annoyed with Mike. He suspected if she'd known Mike wanted to bring visitors to her camp she would have said no. It was awkward, but welcome or not, Ian intended to stay and get his story.

They hiked a quarter of a mile from the camp. Marie didn't want Ian to take any pictures that might identify her location. He agreed to do close-ups only, of a prospector's tent, for example, or a section of ground being checked for indicators.

Every time he focused his camera on a patch of bearberry or Labrador tea, the next thing he knew it had gone wider and found Sarah. In honor of the great outdoors, she wore khakis, a bug jacket, bug hat and hiking shoes. Mike had told the women not to wear makeup—the scent of cosmetics could attract bears—but her eyelashes were thick and dark without help, her lips and cheeks rosy. She and Liz were sticking close together and spending more time on the lookout for predators than for any riches hiding in the ground.

Marie pulled something from her pocket and opened her fingers to show them. It was a rough diamond, about half a carat, Ian guessed.

"No pictures, Ian."

"Sure." He put the camera away.

"I found this stone here, in this exact spot, five years ago. Ever since, I've been looking for its source. Melting glaciers could have swept it here from far away, but my studies suggest it's local. That means there should be diamond-bearing kimberlite in the area. Where there was one diamond, there could be thousands. So far, I've found nothing."

"Isn't there equipment you can have flown over to show you differences in the rock?" Ian asked.

"My budget doesn't stretch that far. I work the old-fashioned way."

"I told you I'd get the money," Mike began, but an intense glare from his fiancée stopped him.

"Um," Sarah said. Ian didn't think he'd ever heard her sound so hesitant. He'd noticed she was being careful not to annoy Marie. "Earlier you said rivers aren't the source. I've been wondering about that."

"Diamonds come from far underground," Marie said. "Really deep down, in the earth's mantle, where there's enough heat and pressure to create them. We'd never be able to dig far enough to reach them. But lucky for us, long ago, here and there across the globe, volcanoes boiled up through the diamond bearing layer."

"Carried the diamonds up to us, you mean?"

"And sprayed them out, like a sneeze," Mike said. "Along with the indicators. So we're looking for the spray area. If we find the pipe and it's rich in diamonds, then we'll be able to interest investors or sell to one of the mining companies." He grinned. "Then we'll get to the 'I dos' at last."

He turned to Marie, his voice quieter, but not enough that the rest of them couldn't hear. "You should stake more claims. Just in case. I looked at the map at the Recording Office. There's a small section on the other side of the lake that no one's taken yet."

"My purse is empty."

"Borrow."

She gritted her teeth. "My purse is empty of borrowed money, too. Do we have to do this in front of others?" She lowered her voice and muttered, "In front of a reporter?"

Walking quickly, they put some distance between themselves and their guests. As far as Ian could tell, they kept on arguing.

"Oh, dear," Liz said.

CHAPTER TWELVE

FOR THE REST OF THE day Mike and Marie ignored each other and paid extra attention to their guests.

Marie agreed to be photographed working with a geologist's hammer and a sieve. Her crouched, lone figure with the lake, the Otter and a winding esker in the background made for an atmospheric shot that told so much of the week's story before Ian typed a word. By the time everyone was dusty and bug-bitten and had shared a meal in the cook tent, the tension level within the group had faded to a tolerable level.

When Marie found out Ian and Sarah's past relationship, she wanted to know more. She started a pot of coffee on top of the stove. "So you were married in college," she said, repeating what Liz had told her, "and within two years you were finished? How did you find each other again?"

"We didn't," Ian said, "not the way you mean. We're just—"

"Working together," Sarah interjected. "We bumped into each other. By chance."

"That makes it fate, doesn't it? Fate wants you together."

"It wasn't chance," Ian said quickly. "Sarah saw my column and decided to come north—"

"So she came looking for you."

"No," Ian and Sarah said together.

"It was an impulse," he added, while she explained that she'd always wanted to see the North, anyway.

Their three listeners nodded. Ian didn't like the pleased looks on their faces. They'd made up their minds romance was in the air.

Sarah tried again to explain. "We bumped into each other in the bar at his hotel. The first thing I saw, before I saw him, was an incredibly ugly moose head hanging on the wall. Then a bunch of old guns and toothy animal traps. Really, not my kind of place. I thought, 'My God, I've walked into a male lair, an honest to goodness Little Red Riding Hood nightmare—'"

"It's not that bad," Ian protested.

"It *is* that bad—"

"It's a sports bar."

"It's a lair. A woman knows a lair when she finds one." She turned to Marie and Liz. "Isn't that right?" They agreed, and she continued, "I tried to look the way people expect me to when they hear I'm a children's book editor. Motherly. Teacherly. Prim. It didn't work. No one who was staring stopped."

Mike grinned. "A woman like you acting prim? A lot of guys have fantasies like that." Ian was glad when Marie slugged him.

"So I stuck as close to Ian as I could for the rest of the evening and no one bothered me."

"Happy ending," Liz said. The next minute she paled at the sound of howling. One voice, then several.

"The caribou herd is on its way back to its winter home in the south," Marie said. "Wolves follow. They won't come through the fence. Anyway, they don't care about us. They have plenty to keep them busy." She went to get the coffeepot, filled mugs for all of them, and put out packaged cookies.

Helping himself to two at once, Mike said, "Tell them about finding the diamond."

How Mike withstood—and ignored—those glares of Marie's, Ian didn't know. Sarah and Liz, who moved closer together on the bench every time the wolves renewed their chorus, protested the story was obviously confidential.

"Off the record?" Ian suggested. He'd got the message a few times over. Marie was worried about other prospectors nosing around. Even if he couldn't use the information, he'd like to hear it.

She fidgeted with her mug. "All right. But if I read your column next week and you—"

"Absolutely not. You won't read anything that bothers you."

She nodded, but he got the feeling she was still deciding whether or not to trust him.

"This is ancestral land of the Dene," she began. "We've seen people come from outside for generations, always looking for riches of some kind. A passage to the Orient for silk and spices. Furs. Gold. Oil. Now diamonds."

"People passing through."

"Sometimes. Sometimes staying." She looked at Mike, not angrily for once. "Mike's great-great-grandfather came here to work at a Hudson's Bay post. But, yeah. Passing through, taking riches with them. That's why I studied geology."

"Keep some riches here."

"When the news about Canadian diamonds first came out, the elders in my village weren't surprised. They told me they'd seen these stones. Going way back, they'd seen them. I asked if they knew where I should begin my search." Marie paused. When she continued she spoke more quietly, as if someone might overhear. "They told me, past the two hills near the lake where the caribou drink."

Ian had noticed two hills from the air, rounded, stony mounds.

"So each summer I camp here, hiking, sifting soil, panning the river." She smiled at Mike.

"That's how we met," he said. "I'd dropped off some hunters up from Texas and on my way home saw this female out in the big, wide Barrens on her own. Thought she needed help, so I landed. And she did need help! She put me to work." He looked at her fondly. "Hasn't stopped, either."

"That's the story he wanted me to tell," Marie said. "Not about the diamond."

"How *did* you find it?" Ian asked.

"As I said. Hiked, sifted, panned. I went where the elders said to go. Sampled here and there. One day there was a glint in the dirt, and that was my diamond." She shook her head. "One little diamond."

"You'll find the pipe," Mike said. "I know you will. A big, beautiful pipe."

THE HOWLING HAD MOVED farther and farther away. By the time the coffee and cookies were finished, the night was quiet.

Liz and Sarah had set up their tent as close

to the biffy as Marie would allow, in case middle-of-the-night trips couldn't be avoided.

Except for the possibility of bears—and wolves, Sarah supposed…and wolverines—it felt like summer camp. They each claimed one side of the nylon floor for their own, arranged sleeping bags and pillows, then changed into flannelette pajamas and zipped themselves into their sleeping bags. The soft light of a camping lantern made the tent seem cozy.

It was important not to rush Liz, but there were only a few days for the North to cure what ailed her. Sarah felt she had to take a hand in the proceedings.

"Liz? I keep thinking about your block. It's so unusual for you. Any ideas about what's getting in your way?"

"I don't need fixing, Sarah."

"We might disagree about that."

"I'm very happy."

"Good. That's wonderful."

Liz laughed. "I mean, there's nothing wrong. Jack is everything I need. He's strong and gentle and funny and smart. He makes me glad every day. And Rose is an easy baby, as babies go."

Sarah didn't know where the envy came from, because she was happy, too. Domesticity had never been one of her goals. She didn't like the feeling, but it stayed there, an ugly knot.

"I'm sorry," Liz added. "Really sorry. I should have told you earlier this week that the book wasn't coming along, but I thought it would be all right. Then the day of the deadline, I couldn't believe it. I didn't have anything."

"Maybe you're too happy."

"All I know is, I can't work."

"Diapers. The dog. The family."

"I'm tired of talking about me. How are you, Sarah?"

"This trip is about you."

"Is it? I thought it was about Ian."

Sarah wanted to deny it, but found she couldn't. "His series, sure."

"You came up here because he needed a fact-checker? That's not very convincing. How are you going to check facts without Internet access or a library or a tourism center?"

It was a good question. "Ian and I didn't think of that."

"How peculiar!"

"An oversight—"

"Can we forget I'm a delinquent writer long enough to figure out what's going on with the two of you?"

"There is no two of us, Liz. We're not

linked. There's just him by himself and then there's me…"

"Do you have any idea how lame a denial that is?"

"Nothing's going on," Sarah said firmly.

"We can talk about it later." Liz unzipped the sleeping bag enough to wriggle out. "Bathroom stop. Coming with me?"

They put on socks and shoes so mosquitoes couldn't attack their feet, and rolled down the mesh in the brim of their bug hats. Pulling warm jackets over their pj's and grabbing flashlights, they crawled outside.

The sun had settled low on the horizon. It bathed the sky and water in an orange light. Under the trees and in the shadows, though, it was black as any night.

"It's like Halloween," Liz said.

Light glowed from the work tent. Sarah heard male voices coming from near the Otter, so she supposed Marie must be there alone. "We're the only ones who went to bed."

"Too eager for a pajama party. Animals can't get into the camp, right?"

"Bells would ring, the fence would zap."

They shone their flashlights on the mossy path to the latrine even though it wasn't really necessary. Inside the tent, they turned on two lanterns that sat beside a washbasin and water jug.

"I thought Three Creeks was isolated," Liz said, from one of the stalls. "Half a mile between houses, a couple of miles to town. Marie is truly on her own. She can't leave unless Mike or somebody comes for her."

Sarah heard a small shriek, then a bump. "Are you all right?"

There were hurried noises, and Liz almost ran from the stall. "A bug." She shook her jacket and the legs of her pajamas, then vigorously batted at her hat. "Is it on me? Sarah? Is it?"

"No." Sarah answered before checking. After a good look she repeated more confidently, "No, there's nothing, Liz. You're fine."

"It was a three inch spider, I'm sure it was. From *The Lord of the Rings* movie set." Liz poured water into the basin and began to wash. "You wouldn't even be able to squish it. There'd be guts everywhere. You'd need a rat trap. I'm not coming back here. Seriously."

"It won't hurt you. Think *Charlotte's Web.*"

"This one's web would say 'amazingly tasty human.'"

Sarah turned her flashlight on and approached the cubicle Liz had abandoned. She pushed the door open with her foot, then peered at the floor, the walls, the corners, the ceiling. She didn't see any rat-size spiders.

Someone knocked on the door. "Hello?" It was Ian. "Am I allowed in? I thought I heard a shout."

"Please!" Liz called back, while Sarah protested in a hiss that she could handle bugs, regardless of their size. "There's a monster spider in here."

Ian looked from Liz to Sarah, hovering outside the stall with her flashlight. "Got it cornered?"

He put his hand out for the light and squeezed past her. She had to admit she was kind of glad to see him. Not *him*. Just someone. Marie could certainly handle whatever Liz had seen. It was her latrine.

"Odd shadows," he said. "Do you think that could be the problem?" He gestured for Liz to come in. She protested, then edged forward and risked peeking where he pointed.

Sarah found room to lean in, too.

The Halloween light from outside projected tree branch shadows onto the wall. An occasional breeze made them dart and stop, lunge and retreat.

Liz backed out of the stall. "I'm so embarrassed."

Ian returned Sarah's flashlight. "We're all a little on edge. If I'd been first in here tonight I would have been the one hollering. Thanks for the heads-up."

Outside, Liz asked, "Did I *holler,* Sarah?"

"Nowhere near. It was a very restrained call of alarm."

"Thank you for saying so." Liz lowered her voice. "He's nice."

"He can be."

Liz was too polite to ask the obvious question, but it hung in the air. *What went wrong?*

Panicking about imaginary spiders while sharing an outhouse had a way of breaking down barriers. Sarah and Liz zipped themselves back into their tent and then their sleeping bags. When Sarah tried one more time to direct the conversation to the Unwritten Book, Liz answered without sounding defensive. Not that her answer was good news.

"Maybe it doesn't have anything to do with my family," she said. "I complain about them sometimes, but I don't want them to be a smaller part of my life. I don't. I just can't find the creative part of me anymore."

"That's a big part to lose."

"My grandmother says having a baby is pretty darn creative."

"Sure. It doesn't help my spring lineup, but if it satisfies you, that's fine." Sarah had meant that to sound understanding, but it didn't at all. "Does it satisfy you?"

"I don't know." Liz turned the lantern lower, then off. "I think it might be gone. Whatever there was that made me see the world as a collection of stories, it's gone."

"It's hibernating."

"I'm different. I'm not just me with a baby. Having a baby changed me."

"Not the core of you."

"Yes, the core of me."

"I don't believe that."

Silence. Then Liz said coolly, "I understand, Sarah. You want a book from me. We have a contract that says you should have one—"

"We have years of a successful partnership that say so. It's not just what I want. This is your career. These are your readers."

"You don't understand. I think about Rose all the time. Dream about her. Wake up trying to put my arms around her even though she's in the next room. Sometimes I think if I don't get time to myself I'll start shouting, bursting, but then if she sleeps too long I miss her, worry about her. Is that crazy?"

Yes seemed like the wrong answer. "Of course

not. I'm sure it's a normal stage of parenting. Maybe this is what you need to write about."

"I don't know if I have another book in me." Liz sounded near tears. "I don't know if I want to do it anymore."

Sarah didn't know what to say.

"It's not the end of the world," Liz insisted. "Jack says it's okay to stop, if that's what I want."

The important phrase being, if that was what she wanted. Sarah didn't believe it was.

"I hope I don't wake up in a panic."

"Because of the bathroom?"

"Because of Rose."

"Jack said she's fine."

"Last night was great at first. No crying, no needs but my own. But then I began to feel panicky before I was even awake. 'Rose, Rose.' Like that. As I woke up it became, 'Where is she? Where's the baby?' My heart was hammering. I thought I'd lost her."

"Oh, Liz."

No wonder she couldn't write or paint. Her mind was dominated by someone else, a literal body-snatching invasion. The baby was more than a drain on her emotional resources. It had replaced writing. Sarah wasn't sure she or the Barrens could offer any competition.

The temperature had fallen since they'd first got ready for sleep. Sarah wriggled deeper into her sleeping bag. When her body sent signals that another trip to the bathroom might be in order, she wriggled even deeper. Mere shadows or not, she wasn't going back to that tent until the sun was well and truly shining.

CHAPTER THIRTEEN

IAN WATCHED SARAH MOVE to a new quadrant. Since morning, they'd been sampling within sight of the camp. Eye the ground, dig, sieve, bag the dirt and take it to Marie for closer examination in the work tent. Mike was off on his own half a football field away, with a hammer and satchel.

He snapped a few shots of her—the smudged slacks, the fatigue. He'd never seen her like this, tired and dirty. For some reason, it touched him.

Because she was a fish out of water, that was why. Unprepared for the heavy work and the rough conditions, and trying not to mind.

Last night, when he'd heard the shout from the latrine, his protective urges had gone through the roof. He was afraid wolves had jumped the electrified wire or that the generator had failed, letting them through.

Scared of shadows, like Liz.

She was digging several yards away from Sarah. The two of them had been keeping their distance from each other since breakfast, when he'd overheard part of a heated discussion about the book Liz hadn't delivered.

He focused the camera on her. She noticed and tugged self-consciously at her oversize shirt, then started toward him.

"I'm afraid Sarah may have sprung me on you, Ian."

"I wouldn't say sprung."

"Thrust? Forced? Pushed?"

"The trip's been constantly evolving. Your addition to it can only be a good thing."

She smiled. "Sarah never mentioned your diplomatic streak. It's interesting to spend time with you. Sort of like hanging out with Mother Goose. You know, someone you didn't think was real."

Why not Han Solo, then? Or Tarzan or even Inspector Gadget? Why *Mother Goose*? "You didn't think I was real?"

"The mythical Husband Number One out from the shadows at last."

"Husbands Two and Three aren't mythical?"

"Not to me. I met them both, briefly."

He tried to resist his curiosity, but failed. "What were they like?"

"They seemed nice. Not as nice as you."

He smiled. She was probably being polite. They stood side by side, looking harder at the tundra the longer the silence went on. Ian wasn't sure what else to say to this person from Sarah's professional life. It was a part of her he had trouble envisioning.

"I hear you're suffering from writer's block."

"Actually, I'm not suffering. I'm quite happy not to be writing. Sarah is suffering, though."

Her offhand manner gave him a glimpse of the problem Sarah faced. "You promised her a book."

"And Jack a wife. Rose, a mom."

"Your house a cleaner, your garden a weeder…"

Liz smiled. "The cucumbers a pickler, the plums a jammer."

"You do all that, in this day and age? You can get pickles and jam at the store, you know."

"Ever see crabapple–plum–Nanking cherry jam at the store?"

"Maybe not."

"I'll send you a jar. You'll see there are worse things not to make than a book."

"I know what Sarah would say."

"Write the damn book?"

"She'd say, let someone else in your family make that lovely jam. Only you can write one of your books."

The weight of the world might as well have come down on Liz's shoulders. "You know what that sounds like to me? As if you're saying that's all I can do, all I'm allowed to do. What if jam is my heart's desire? Oh, I know," she said quickly, before he had a chance to reply, "I don't have a contract to make jam."

"Is that the refrain you hear? That you've got a contract?"

"It's more like 'got to, got to, got to.'"

Ian grimaced sympathetically. "And we all know how imagination thrives on guilt and panic."

Liz laughed. "You remind me of Jack. You're a good listener, too." Her amusement faded, leaving her with a sad expression. "Do you know if there's a way I can call home?"

"Marie has a satellite phone in the work tent."

Liz brightened. "Thanks so much!" Taking her tools with her, she hurried back to camp.

"EVERYTHING ALL RIGHT?" Sarah called to Ian, when she saw Liz take off.

One hand to his ear, he made dialing motions with the other.

Again?

Liz had phoned Jack as soon as she'd reached Yellowknife, then in the morning before the flight, and during lunch. Sarah supposed it was heartwarming, but she couldn't help feeling that Liz was sabotaging her own road trip, her own escape.

Sarah flexed her knees, then sat on the ground to rest them. Ian had been snapping photos and writing in a notebook all day. She loved watching him when he was intent on work.

The attraction she felt for him confused her. Attraction itself confused her. When she saw a man who made her heart beat faster, she wanted him for her own. And no one had ever made her heart beat faster than Ian did.

But at some point a person's heart rate had to return to normal, and then what?

Then it was over.

What about her parents? They'd been married for forty years. Maybe it wasn't about attraction for them. They certainly cared about each other; that was obvious every day. But maybe they had more of a partnership, some sort of calm mutual appreciation. Maybe attraction was a warning, a pain signal Sarah misinterpreted, while other, wiser people like her parents knew it meant to back away.

Ian capped his camera and put his pen in his pocket. She watched him walk across the field toward her and didn't feel the slightest wish to back away.

"Writer's retreat not going well?" he asked.

"She'll be all right."

"You mean productive."

"I hope so. I annoyed her this morning."

Amusement flashed across his face. "Only this morning?"

"She didn't want to hear my suggestions. A non-fiction book about a Dene geologist, for example. Or something closer to home. Her husband grows Christmas trees and pumpkins. How about, *A Day in the Life of a Christmas Tree Farmer.* Or a story based on her family. *Grandma on the Farm.* Most children grow up in the city these days. She could teach them something important. But she says that isn't what the kids expect from her. She's had enough of the kind of story she usually writes, but she won't try anything new."

"She didn't ask you for inspiration."

Did he mean that he agreed with Liz, that it was unreasonable to push for a story, any story? "You do see that this is a problem, don't you? If you suddenly decided not to finish your series for the Globe, would that be okay with anyone?"

His expression became more serious. "No, it wouldn't."

"She thinks she's finished as a writer. I don't believe it. If anything, as Rose begins to discover the world ideas will flow faster than Liz can catch them. But she's been in a broody hen phase. You know? Her energies are devoted to nesting."

"Her life is in turmoil. You must have experienced that. A dramatic change that leaves you questioning everything?"

"I try to move forward. Why get bogged down? It doesn't help."

"Bogged down," he repeated.

He didn't seem to like her choice of words, so she changed the subject. "I was watching you work. Were you writing your column?"

"Getting some ideas down."

"It reminds me of the way I used to imagine our life." She smiled. "Not the dirt and the bugs, but both of us involved with writing. Except I always thought you'd write fiction. Be the Shakespeare of our time."

"That was never going to happen."

"You never tried."

He sighed, frustrated or annoyed, or both. "That was your dream, not mine, Sarah. I don't even know where you got the idea."

"From you. From the way you talked in class. You were so smart and so…passionate about the poems we read, the ideas in them." She laughed, remembering. "Then there was your hair."

"My hair?"

"All dark and curly and poufy—"

"Hey!"

"In the manliest possible way. I thought you looked like Lord Byron."

"And that made me the next Shakespeare? Sarah, you've got a drastic way with logic."

"I make the connections. I get from A to B."

Her poet that never was. All those curly-locked guys in ruffled shirts—she'd been so sure, years ago, that he fit right in with them.

Now she couldn't remember why she'd considered curls and ruffles good things. Jeans, a slightly unshaven look and a bit of an edge certainly had appeal, too. So did his all-grown-up body, with muscles he couldn't have built if he'd stayed too close to a computer keyboard or a pencil.

The poet image wasn't all a fantasy. He *had* whispered poems in her ear.

Like the day they took the canoe out on the river. She had persuaded him to paddle while she lounged in the bow, her head on a cushion, reading Shakespeare's sonnets. At first they had to endure catcalls from her brothers on shore, but when they were far enough away no one could ruin her pleasure.

She had rested the book on her lap, her mind full of similes and metaphors and flowery thoughts. "Ian, compare me to a summer's day. Really. I'm not joking. Am I more lovely and more temperate?"

"Maybe not temperate."

That had pleased her. Eighteen-year-olds weren't aiming for temperance. "Not cool and foggy and drizzly, though, I'll bet."

"Foggy, sometimes."

She'd given him a gentle kick and the canoe had rocked dangerously.

"Sunny, but stormy," he elaborated, "with occasional bouts of fog."

"How romantic. You'll never rival Shakespeare with lines like that."

"Writers aren't allowed to be romantic these days. Too much irony in the air."

"I'll allow it."

He'd laid the oar on the bottom of the canoe, taken hold of the gunnels, and, hand over hand, rocking the craft like a cradle, found his way to her. He'd whispered in her ear something with a Shakespearean rhythm. She couldn't hear a word. For all she knew it had been some variation of roses are red, violets are blue. That didn't matter. All that mattered were his lips at her ear, his body over hers, his eyes laughing.

"Sarah?"

"Um?" Her mind was still faraway.

"Daydreaming or worrying?"

"I don't even know anymore."

CHAPTER FOURTEEN

WHEN THE SUN REACHED its lowest point on their last night at the camp, Marie made a fire using some of her supply of dead wood. Mike said he needed to do a mechanical check on the Otter and Ian wanted to write his column, so it was just the three women.

They spread blankets on the ground to sit on, and Sarah unpacked the wine she'd been waiting for the right opportunity to drink. She decided this was the time.

She held up the bottle for the others to see. "Oliver gave me this."

"Fraser Press Oliver?" Liz asked.

"The same. As a gift when Jared and I were married. Not a wedding gift, but as something extra for me. The note said to open it on a special occasion well into the marriage, when I'd forgotten to wonder if it was going to last this time."

"Ouch."

Sarah shrugged. "How many people get a chance to look for gems so close to the arctic circle? That's worth celebrating."

Marie excused herself and returned moments later with a bottle of her own. "Brandy from Mike. An emergency bottle for if I fall into a freezing lake."

The flames and smoke did a fairly good job of keeping the bugs away. Sarah opened the wine and, accompanied by the crackling of the fire, they drank to diamond-bearing kimberlite, rough diamonds and diamonds cut and polished.

"I have three, you know," Sarah said. "A great, big, beautiful life insurance policy of a stone from Jared, a more modest but charmingly cut antique stone from Derek—" she reached under her shirt and pulled out the chain that held her first engagement ring "—and this little sweetie from Ian."

"Thrice blessed," Marie said.

"That's what I'll tell my brothers next time they rib me."

"Is that it, Sarah? Are you done trying?"

"Done and done and done."

"She doesn't mean it," Liz said. "She's a true optimist. She thinks being here will help me write a book."

"You're the optimist. You're in it for the long

haul. You went so far as to have a child." Sarah looked through the shadows to Marie. "How long have you been with Mike?"

"Not long. Five years."

"Neck and neck with Liz. I'm good at starting relationships...."

"Well, hey, aren't we all. Falling in love is the easy part, Sarah. Staying there is another matter."

"That's what I haven't been able to figure out. What do you do after riding into the sunset? The curtain always closes then, you know?"

"You wash the dishes," Liz said.

Marie nodded, laughing. "Rinse and repeat."

"Then maybe I'm right to keep away from sunsets." Sarah held her ring, her first ring, to the light of the fire. The stone was too small to reflect the flames, or maybe it wasn't well cut.

She slid it on her finger, thinking of the day Ian had put it there. "We got engaged during spring term, first year university. Got married that summer."

"You were babies," Marie said.

"It was his idea. He always claims I'm the impulsive one."

"How did he pop the question?"

She smiled, remembering. It was years since she'd thought of that day. "Everybody else in my family had gone to the cottage. I didn't go because of exams, so I was lonely and feeling sorry for myself."

Marie and Liz were nodding. Sarah realized they'd been much farther than that from their families when they went to school. Ian had been, too.

"You must think I was a brat."

They protested that they didn't.

"What happened?" Marie asked. "You were lonely, so Ian proposed?"

"I hope that wasn't why. Not exactly a solid foundation." She refilled the three glasses, wondering uneasily if Marie had hit on the problem. Ian couldn't have just been sorry for her.

"That wasn't why," Liz said. She sounded very sure. "Look at you, you gorgeous thing. I'll bet he wanted you the first day he saw you."

He had. He'd told her so. They'd wanted each other.

"Anyway," Sarah went on, "I complained about not being able to hear the loon that nested at the lake. So Ian took me to a museum, a science museum with nature displays, and hurried me past the bison and the giant sloth. I didn't know why we'd bothered paying admission just to rush through like that. We didn't stop till we reached a loon exhibit. A recording of its call was playing. So haunting. So real."

"That was sweet of him," Marie said.

"Then he pulled out a little box, that engagement ring box that makes you say, 'Oh, my God,' as soon as you see it. So I started to cry and said yes before he asked." Her throat tightened.

Liz put a hand on her arm. "Aw, Sarah—"

"That's okay. Really, I'm not sad about the course of things. It's bittersweet, though, to think of the time before the mistakes. And I've made a few."

Marie raised her glass. "To mistakes. Because in our mistakes we see our true nature."

"That sounds awfully bleak."

"But then we learn," Liz said, "and improve our natures."

Marie shook her head. "Not me."

"Me, neither." Sarah proposed another toast. "To mistakes that teach us and mistakes that don't."

COMING OUT OF THE WORK tent where he'd been using Marie's generator as a power source for his laptop, Ian saw Mike leave the Otter and head out to the exploration area. The women were still by the fire, their voices flowing and blending in a way that suggested sisterhood. He decided to follow Mike.

Every now and then the outfitter disappeared from view, then he'd go up an incline and Ian would see him silhouetted against the sky again. Soon they were outside the area Marie had asked them to sample. Ian began to wonder where Mike was headed, and why. It was late for a stroll.

He was about to turn around, thinking he was too far behind to catch up, when he heard a scuffling noise. He froze. No gun, no stick. All he had was his camera. The flash? Maybe.

It didn't sound like an animal. He edged forward, around the base of a hill, the spicy scent of Labrador tea rising as he brushed against vegetation.

Mike was standing in a circle of lantern light, kicking at the ground with the toe of his boot.

"I guess you can almost work through the night in the summer," Ian said.

Mike whirled around, nearly falling over. "F—"

"Sorry about that."

"Jeez. What if I thought you were a grizzly?"

"A talking grizzly?"

Mike gave a twisted smile. "Well, it wouldn't matter how much of an idiot I felt like after shooting you, would it? You'd still be shot."

"Point taken. Giving it one more try before you go?"

Mike was still off balance. "Yeah, I've got a hunch about this area."

Ian remembered him saying something the day they'd arrived at the camp about a triangular piece of land he thought was promising. This must be it.

"Marie's methodical," Mike said. "She won't look in one zone until she's completely done with another. I say if you've sampled half a quadrant and come up empty, the other half is likely to treat you the same."

"I'd help, but you don't seem to have any tools."

"I didn't say I'd formed a plan." Mike sounded sheepish.

Strange that Sarah's impulsiveness annoyed Ian and Mike's made him laugh. "You're not the methodical one."

"Airline pilots are methodical. Bush pilots fix planes and people with gum and elastic bands. It's a seat-of-the-pants life."

Hardly needing to look at his camera, Ian adjusted the aperture for the available light. He pointed and clicked. *That's the picture,* he thought, *and that's the quote.*

THEY'D BEEN TOASTING WITH the brandy for a while now. Sarah was pretty sure they'd covered the same ground more than once, but the fog in her head made it difficult to be sure. She'd never been a very good drinker.

Husbands were on her mind. Multiples of husbands.

"They all seemed like such great guys. Well, they were, they are. Great guys. Attractive, funny, smart. What more could I want?"

Liz shrugged. "Something, obviously. Something was missing."

"Three tries!" Sarah emphasized the number by holding up some fingers, peering at them to make sure she'd got it right. "And I'm not even old. Three tries in ninety years, okay. But three tries in twelve years? That's not love. How can that be love?"

"You've got a big heart?" Liz suggested.

Sarah snorted. "Generous. If you've got it, share it." It was meant to be a joke, but tears sprang to her eyes. She blinked and swallowed, then raised her voice to intimidate any errant emotions. "Maybe I don't believe in love. Romance, either. Canoes and poems, no. If anyone tries to compare you to a summer's day, run."

"I wouldn't mind being compared to a summer's day," Marie said.

Liz just smiled. She had Jack, with his

summer-perfect blueberries, Halloween pumpkins and Christmas trees, for heaven's sake. What could be more romantic than that? No wonder she wasn't taking time to write. Sarah wouldn't work, either, if she lived on a fairy-tale farm.

Try as she might, she couldn't hold on to her sense of celebration. It was sad that her special bottle of wine was gone, shared with an author she'd alienated and a geologist she wouldn't see again, at a time when she'd dis-interred the bones of her first and best marriage and was carrying them around for all to see. Why did she keep on thinking good things would happen? She made one blunder after another.

Marie had thought of another toast. "Friends old and new."

Definitely. You definitely needed friends when you were lousy at love. Sarah drank to friends, then said, "To you, Marie. To your mine. To your dreams." She heard the men re-turning from wherever they'd gone, so she lifted her glass again. "And to close encounters of the masculine kind."

"You had to go and say that," Liz said sadly. "Now I'm homesick."

THE FIRE WAS OUT AND THEY'D all gone to their respective sleeping bags.

Sarah couldn't stop talking. Liz kept telling her to hush. She tried to lower her voice, but it went louder again on its own. She had no volume control.

Anyway, she didn't want to hush. She wanted to lie in the almost dark, talking to a girlfriend. When had she last done that—when she was fifteen? People needed to talk to girlfriends. Girlfriends understood and told you you were right.

So she explained again why she'd come north and what her first conversation with Ian in ten years had been like, while Liz—more of a really friendly female colleague than a girlfriend—alternated *uh-huh* with *shh*.

Until she said, "You didn't."

The change in her response pattern made Sarah be quiet and think. "Didn't what?"

"You and Ian had sex?"

"We made love."

"It was a one-night stand. You had sex."

"You're supposed to understand."

"I do. Are you *trying* to get hurt?"

Okay, Sarah thought, sometimes girlfriends—and female colleagues—lectured. Kindly, because they understood so well. "Of course not. Maybe it wasn't the best thing to do. We sort of fell down a rabbit hole."

Liz told her she was talking too loud and would wake the others, so Sarah wriggled closer to Liz's side of the tent, taking her sleeping bag with her.

In a loud whisper, she stated, "There we were, Liz, virtual strangers, which was a very odd feeling in itself, and then next thing we knew we were making love just like we used to, as if it was right, as if we belonged together."

"Sarah, you're shouting in my ear, and if Ian isn't sound asleep I promise he can hear, too."

"I'm not shouting." She didn't think she was, anyway. She tried to talk more quietly. "It was wonderful. It's never been as wonderful with anyone else. I mean, I'm sorry for the whole rest of womankind that not everyone can experience Ian at his best. Tender and fierce, sensitive, you know? The guy knows his way around a woman's body—"

"I don't need to hear the whole story, Sarah. I've got the idea."

"But then, so quickly, we were climbing out of the rabbit hole and we went back to being strangers, awkward and wondering what we'd just done."

"Poor Sarah."

"Now he ignores me. Except when he's being mean to me."

"He isn't mean to you, Sarah."

"He's *so* mean to me! He's nice to everybody else."

"And you want to fall back into the rabbit hole with him anyway."

"Occasional visits, I'm thinking."

"Why? Do you still love him?"

Hadn't she explained? Tender, fierce, sensitive. Did Liz need another reason? "Of course not."

"You're sure?"

"We rode into the sunset for about three minutes and then it went wrong. I don't know what happened. He changed, that's what." Foggy pictures came to mind. "He was so romantic, so full of ideas and poetry, so full of questions and dreams. And then all of a sudden he was no fun anymore. Just, 'Oh, that costs too much, it's too late, go to sleep, be serious. No, Sarah, no, Sarah,' over and over...! Are you laughing?"

"No...a little bit. It's a little bit funny when you do his voice. Sarah, I don't want to tell you *no, no, no,* but really. You can't flirt with your ex-husband. You'll both get hurt."

"And you're an expert in this sort of thing, Little Miss Three Creeks?"

"Sarah, go to sleep. Get off my foot and go to sleep."

"Is that your foot? I'm sorry, Liz, really, I thought it was a rock. Did I hurt it? It isn't sprained or anything? Crushed?"

"It's fine."

"You know what? I'm going to go talk to Ian—"

Hands grabbed her and pulled her to the ground. "Go to sleep, Sarah. Lie down. Head on the pillow."

"Bossy."

"Take a deep breath," Liz said soothingly. "Let it out. And every time you exhale, put away any thoughts in your mind."

"Ian is a jerk. He said so himself."

"Exhale and put it out of your mind."

Sarah tried, but it rushed right back in. "It isn't working."

"Patience."

Liz breathed in and out with her, talking her through the process like an air traffic controller. Sarah told her that, but she ignored the interruption, her voice slowing and becoming a mumble. Soon it was clear she'd fallen asleep.

Hard ground must not pose any challenge after months of middle-of-the-night feedings. Sarah tried not to toss and turn. A sound sleep might mean inspiration for Liz the next day. She didn't want to toy with that. There was no point tossing and turning, anyway. One rock wasn't any softer than the next.

She was beginning to regret talking so openly by the fire. She'd made herself look ridiculous. Three marriages, three short, sad marriages. The only conclusion people could come to was that there was something wrong with her. She was shallow, she couldn't commit, she was a sex addict. She knew people said those things. None of them were true. She didn't defend herself. People thought what they wanted to think.

Her brothers were kinder. They said she was an optimist, try, try, try again. If she saw a man she liked, according to them, she married him.

She played along, saying that since she didn't want to cheat or sleep around, divorce and re-marriage were her only options. They must know, didn't they, that she didn't really believe that? Each time she married she hoped it was forever, that there would be some special alchemy that made it work.

But the magic went out of it so quickly. Was she supposed to live without magic? Maybe if she was religious, if she believed in some kind of eternal bliss, it would be different. As far as she knew, this was it. If she wasn't happy or fulfilled now, when would she be?

Sarah listened to Liz's breathing, shallow, rhythmic, untroubled, until her own eyes became heavy and she pushed the word *jerk* out of her mind one last time.

CHAPTER FIFTEEN

SARAH STUMBLED TO the cook tent the next morning, unable to look at, or speak to, anyone. She took a mug of coffee away from the group and found a secluded, sun-warmed rock to sit on. Soon she heard stones crunching. Footsteps. The sound hurt her head.

Ian prised the mug from her hand and replaced it with a bottle of water. She peered at him through half-closed eyes.

"If I ever needed caffeine, it's now."

"Caffeine dehydrates. You're already dehydrated. Water will help your head."

"My head's fine."

"Humor me." He handed her two tablets. "Take those."

She obeyed, doubting they'd do any good. "I never drink like that." Dimly, she realized she'd just denied having a headache, too. "Really, I don't." She remembered some of her conversation with Liz. Her loud conversation. Had Ian heard any of it?

He went away, taking her coffee with him.

At least it was quiet here. Not a single motor. No sirens, no telephone, no doorbell. Just the murmur of voices and the occasional burst of birdsong.

But after lunch it was time to move to the next location and silence ended in a big way.

Sarah huddled in the back of the Otter, vaguely aware of tundra being replaced by a wide expanse of water. She heard Mike say they were over Great Bear Lake. Then he called out, as excited as a kid, that they had crossed the arctic circle.

At last. The pleasure of it got through Sarah's haze. She smiled at Liz. "We've done it. Reached the frozen North." Sled dogs, belugas and dear old elves.

Mike's grin somehow got wider. "There's the herd!"

Sarah risked a look out the window. Far below, a dark mass against the gray and red of the ground, a barren-ground caribou herd, thousands strong, moved like one huge creature. People said the herd flowed like a river. Except unlike a river, it changed course halfway through the year and began flowing the other way.

The thought was almost too much for Sarah's stomach. To her horror, Mike dipped a wing to give them a better view. She moaned and clutched the sick bag.

Ian turned from the front seat. "We're nearly there."

That was the best news ever.

Mike zeroed in on a rocky outcropping, a finger of land where stunted jack pines had found enough soil to grow. He circled twice—checking for signs the area might be home to bears, he told them—before landing. The plane bobbed on the water. Sarah couldn't hold back another quiet moan. Feeling airsick and seasick all at once wasn't fair.

Liz patted her leg. "There, there."

"Very comforting, Mom. Why are *you* fine?"

"Made of sterner stuff than you, I guess. Come on, you can curl up in the moss and I'll help the guys make camp."

Sarah wasn't about to accept that degree of uselessness. She and Liz set up their tent again, far enough from Mike's and from Ian's that any wildlife that wandered into camp wouldn't feel hemmed in. Hemmed in wildlife tended to panic, Mike told them, which could involve charging, stomping, goring, biting.... Fortunately, he had a trip wire to put around the tents.

Not electrified, like Marie's permanent system, but enough to discourage animals and warn humans. As a last and important precaution, he and Ian suspended the food supply high off the ground between two of the pine trees.

By then, Liz had wandered off. Sarah saw her following the lakeshore, climbing up and down smooth, worn rocks. Ian had his camera out and Mike was tinkering with the plane, so Sarah finally did stretch out on a mossy bit of ground. She closed her eyes.

With her bug gear on, it wasn't exactly sunbathing, but it was restful. The sounds of buzzing insects and lapping water soothed her.

She must have fallen asleep. She had no sense of how much time had passed, but over the sounds of buzzing and lapping, she now heard voices. Mike and Ian were beside a propane stove, set up on a flat boulder outside the trip-wired area. Steam rose from a pot.

Ian brought her an enameled mug of tea. "Better now?"

"Sheepish."

"What got into you, Sarah?"

She shrugged. Among the three of them the wine hadn't gone far. The brandy might have been unwise. "I didn't drink any more than the others."

"You never did have a head for alcohol. You worry me, Sarah. I keep getting the feeling there's something you're going to tell me, like you have a terrible disease or we had a child you've neglected to mention."

"I'm as healthy as an ox and all I've got is Jenny." His concern made her uncomfortable. The subject needed to be changed. "Poor Liz. I've ignored her since last night."

"She hasn't minded. She's in a daze."

Sarah brightened. "Really? With a faraway expression and a sketch pad?"

"A faraway expression, anyway."

"It's a start."

"Any backup plan if she doesn't come through?"

"She will come through. You've only met Liz McKinnon, the obsessed and sleepy mother. I know Elizabeth Robb."

MIKE HAD ANNOUNCED THEY were going to catch their dinner. The two men actually fished, but Sarah only cast a hookless line for the pleasure of it, and Liz sat off by herself doing something that looked remarkably like sketching.

It didn't take Mike and Ian long to catch enough fish, a pickerel and three grayling.

Sarah hadn't seen an actual grayling before, only a fillet on a plate. Their dorsal fins were like small sails, and a thin line of pink along their sides flashed in the light. At first she couldn't look away from their beauty and then she couldn't watch their pain. Later, after they were fried over an open fire, she had to admit they were delicious.

Liz still seemed distant after dinner. Sarah hoped in her clumsy attempt to inspire a book she hadn't done permanent damage to their friendship. Knowing when to leave well enough alone and when to try harder was always a challenge for her.

They walked along the stony beach, away from the tethered plane.

"Did I drag you up here, Liz?"

"Kind of."

"And I've been really heavy-handed."

Liz didn't deny it, but at least she smiled. "Being up here is giving me a chance to think."

"Good. I'm glad."

"I spent fifteen years avoiding my home because of what happened to Andy." Her first husband. "Fifteen years! That's a big chunk of my life."

"You didn't waste those years. You built your career."

"While avoiding everything else. Now I'm married and have a child and live in Three Creeks again." She stopped. She sounded as if she couldn't put her finger on what was bothering her.

"Too much?" Sarah guessed. "Too much change all at once?"

"Wonderful change."

Sarah nodded. Reconciled with friends and family, a new love, a child. What was the problem, then? "I wish I understood. Are you afraid you're missing something, the way you did during those fifteen years? From the outside, your life seems complete."

"It does, doesn't it? The only thing missing is the book." Liz sounded calm, when she began, but her voice tightened as she went on. "So what do I let go? What part of it should I not value? Playing with Rose? The sliver of time Jack and I have after she falls asleep at night? Sundays with the Robbs? Tea with my grandmother? What should go?"

Sarah didn't have the answer. "Forget my spring list for a minute, Liz. Forget the contract. Remember who you are. You see life in images and the images tell you a story. That's how your mind works. Is that a part you shouldn't value?"

"So much useless mulling." Liz tried to smile. "While Fraser Press waits."

"Fraser Press can take it. Mull all you need to."

Liz's eyes glistened. "Thank you, Sarah."

She'd finally said the right thing. Too bad it didn't solve the problem.

They turned and began walking back to the camp. Small in the distance, Mike was tending to the Otter and farther along the peninsula Ian was taking photos, close-ups, it seemed, of vegetation. Everywhere they walked the same plants grew, Labrador tea, with its glossy leaves and tiny white flowers, and bearberry, which turned a beautiful red in late summer. There were others, but those were the two Sarah could identify.

"I don't know what Ian keeps finding to photograph," she said. "For miles, everything looks the same."

"Maybe when he shows you the photos you'll see what he sees."

"He won't be showing me."

"No?" Liz looked at Sarah curiously. "Still denying your connection? Even after the things you said last night?"

"I was hoping you wouldn't remember any of that." After a minute, Sarah said, "It's been confusing seeing him, but when I decided to come up here it was because of someone else."

Liz was surprised enough to stop walking. "You're going out with someone new?"

"I'm considering it." They resumed walking. "He's Jenny's vet. Brent. I like the name. So straightforward, no fuss. He's sweet with her, Liz. Watching them together I turn to mush. Isn't that what we all like, a gentle guy who's good with animals and children?"

"You're falling for him because he's good with your dog?"

Sarah nodded. "But then I thought, am I really going to do this again? Throw my heart over the fence and then fall off the other side? Because if I let myself like this guy, next thing I know we'll be married and next thing after that it'll be over."

"Sarah. Honey. No."

"Yes. That's what always happens."

"Have you considered not jumping? Stepping carefully?"

"Going slowly to my doom?"

Liz laughed. "If I understand you, you've run to Ian so he'll save you from asking Brent the Vet out on a date? And therefore, from another disastrous marriage?"

Sarah couldn't help laughing, too. "Something like that."

Liz shook her head, a little theatrically for Sarah's liking, as if trying to clear her thoughts. "Any chance you give up on your relationships too quickly?"

"Work at it, you mean? Love shouldn't be work. It should soar." Liz didn't answer. "Is that silent disapproval?"

"I'm thinking. It can soar, Sarah, but sometimes it plods along. Sometimes it breaks down and needs care—"

A shout coming from the peninsula stopped her. They saw Mike leaning out of the plane's cockpit, and Ian hurrying to join him.

"That was a happy shout, wasn't it?" Sarah asked. "Not a plane is broken and we're stranded shout?"

Mike whooped and banged Ian on the back, then looked around until he saw them. He waved, an exuberant sweep of his arm.

"A happy shout," Liz said.

MARIE'S CALL HAD COME in over Mike's radio. At first Ian hadn't understood what she was saying, but he'd heard excitement in her voice. Great excitement.

Mike hadn't understood, either. "Say again?"

There was static, and then the word "garnets."

A slow mile had spread over Mike's face. "Hang on, sweetheart. Did you say you've found garnets?" He'd let out a whoop, and two ducks on the lake took off in alarm.

"Okay, okay, tell me again. Where?" He

grinned at Ian and then past him, at Liz and Sarah hurrying along the beach to join them. "That little strip? I *told* you to look there, didn't I?" He spoke in an aside to Ian. "I told her last summer."

Garnets on the triangular strip, Ian thought. Well, people always said you found things in the last place you looked.

CHAPTER SIXTEEN

MIKE'S PASSENGERS thought he should turn the plane around so he could go celebrate with Marie, but he said he had a business to run, too, and his customers had paid to see the Arctic Ocean.

So in the morning they flew west, returning to the Mackenzie River, which they'd first seen at Fort Simpson three days before. They rejoined it much farther north, over Fort Good Hope, and soon were in sight of the delta. It was a dizzying, gauzy expanse of green and blue. Islands of silt gave trees a place to grow, swans a nesting ground and carved the huge river into winding channels and lakes.

Ian's camera never stopped clicking. What pleased Sarah most was how alert and watchful Liz had become, how silent. The North had at last captured her imagination.

They flew to the end of the delta, to Tuktoy-aktuk, a hamlet on the coast. There, they walked right down to the shore and, as Mike had promised, put their toes in the icy water.

"Where's the North Pole?" Liz asked, looking out to sea, her voice distant.

"Depends which one you want," Mike said. "The real one, that's far away. The magnetic one is closer, near the Queen Elizabeth Islands."

That reminded Sarah of her joking conversation with Ian about a North Pole expedition. The minute she thought of it, an idea began to grow. An image of a child, a little girl with tousled morning hair and flannelette pajamas, on skis maybe, surrounded by unending drifts of snow.

Smiling, she turned to Liz and proceeded to tell her all about it, adding that the girl was no doubt searching for Santa, for Santa's North Pole.

"It would be a great story, wouldn't it? Not a spring story—"

"Sarah," Ian said quietly. "Don't."

She tensed. He was always telling her "don't."

Quietly enough that the others wouldn't hear, he said, "You have to leave her alone. You brought her here. Now let her be."

IAN SUGGESTED THEY WALK together and, unusually silent, Sarah agreed. He didn't know if she was stunned by what he'd said or by the desolate beauty of the coast.

"I guess I was pushing Liz."

"I guess you were."

"That was good, that you stopped me. I mean, I hate it when you do that, but Liz seems to be thinking about an idea of her own, doesn't she? I don't want to interfere with that."

They stopped to watch seals on an island not far offshore.

"Was it like this where you grew up in Churchill, Ian?"

"Similar. Shield, straggly trees and tundra, a big body of cold water. Belugas swim in the bay, too, and feed at the mouth of the Churchill River. They're a common sight in summer."

"Why didn't we ever go see them?"

"That's quite the selective memory you've got, Sarah."

"I don't know what you mean."

"My parents kept asking us to visit. You always had an excuse."

"Did I?"

"Exams, the cottage, the distance, the cost." Even after all this time, repeating the list made the old tension come back. "None of that was untrue, but the bottom line was you weren't interested."

"I'm sorry, Ian."

She sounded sincere. He warmed to her right

away. Amazing what that short and simple phrase could do. "When I was a kid I thought we lived on top of the world. I thought I should be able to see all of it—look down that curve of the planet to Africa or South America."

Sarah laughed.

"I wasn't a very smart kid."

"You were a sweet kid. Did you try using binoculars?"

He nodded. "My dad's. Then a telescope. It must have been short on power because still no pyramids, no lions, no savannah. Nothing but water or ice or snow or tundra, depending on the season and the direction."

"But now you've been to Africa. You've seen the pyramids."

"And the lions."

"And came home to water and tundra."

"Funny how that happens. People end up drawn to the very things they couldn't wait to escape. I could have proposed any series of articles to the *Globe*. I wanted to come here."

"You know what I find really interesting?" She moved closer to him and had a gleam in her eye, so he suspected it had nothing to do with travel or childhood views of the world. "Even though you're ten years older and two husbands have been and gone—"

She was going to drive him crazy. "No, you don't, Sarah."

"Don't what?"

"Whatever it is you're doing."

"All I'm doing is finding you interesting." She said it so innocently, but she was clearly enjoying herself. "And this spark—"

"There's no spark."

"It's still there. Why else did we race to your hotel room? You can't deny it was…pretty spectacular."

"I don't."

"Maybe we should be lovers, sporadically, if we find ourselves in the same town, and leave it at that."

"Or not."

"Not leave it?"

"Not get into it. I try to learn from my mistakes."

IAN WAS RIGHT. PLAYING WITH each other's feelings wouldn't end well.

She'd loved his openness talking about his childhood in Churchill. It made her ideas about him shift, like slides in a projector, the kind her dad used to have, individually loaded, clicking back and forth, changing views. Not this picture, the poet, but that one, the curious traveler.

"Didn't I know you?" She heard a touch of longing in her voice. She didn't want him to get the impression it mattered more than it did. "I don't like to think my perceptions were unreliable."

"Maybe you didn't pay close enough attention to perceive accurately."

That stung. "Was I hard to live with, Ian?"

He didn't answer for what felt like five minutes. The delay made his eventual reply unconvincing. "No."

No? That was all? "What, then? You preferred not to live with me? It was as simple as that?"

"Can I change my answer?"

"I'm serious."

"We don't need to be serious."

"But I want to know."

"All right. Yes. You were hard to live with."

Sarah began walking, in no particular direction, just not where he was. She wanted distance. Come to think of it, she wanted lots of distance.

"Sarah, you wanted an answer. I didn't mean to hurt you."

"You didn't hurt me."

"I see that." Now he sounded impatient. On top of all the rest. He thought she was impulsive and thoughtless, imperceptive and hasty, emotionally blind. Why had he married her? Well, that was easy. The bonking was just so good.

He grabbed her by the arm and pulled her to a stop, then around to face him. She wouldn't. She stared at the ground and tried not to see his feet. She didn't want to see him at all.

"You can't flounce around like that, Sarah. This is a wild place. This is where polar bears live."

The main thing she heard was flounce. *Flounce*. Nothing could have summarized his opinion of her better than that. How did he despise her, let her count the ways.

"I don't flounce," she said, in a small, tight voice. "But you have aggravated me beyond reason."

"I don't tell you fairy tales. You've never liked that, but somebody has to pay attention."

"To what? Bills, the dark, germs?"

"For a start."

His arrogance was unbelievable. "You think I don't? What, do you think I have a nanny? I pay my bills. I turn off and on the lights and I wash my hands before I eat."

She got closer, leading with her chin. She was so mad. Steaming. "How long did I live with you? *Two years*. Two. That's nothing but a sliver of my life. And guess what? I've survived the rest of it without you there shaking your finger at me."

"When did I shake my finger? I never did."

"Every single day!" At the back of her mind she knew it wasn't true, but she couldn't stop herself from saying it. And even as she listened to the lie, she heard herself repeating it. "Every single day. And I've had enough."

He let go of her arm. "You and me both."

Her anger faded. Sarah ached, thinking of who he'd been for that short while when they were young. Without any warning, he'd changed. She'd tried to remind him, tried to bring back the…the fun of that first year. The sense of possibility, the wonder, the maybe. She loved *maybe*. She'd loved his expression when he'd talked about all the things they might do.

"I loved you," she said.

"You thought you did."

Where was the *Me, too?* "You're so much nicer to everyone else."

"It's easier to be nice to everyone else."

She closed her eyes against the pain of that. They were done. If it wasn't completely over ten years ago, it was completely over now. She walked around him, keeping him at arm's length, sick of the Arctic, sick of belugas, sick of bugs and diamonds and the frigging North Pole. She wanted to go home.

CHAPTER SEVENTEEN

IF NOT FOR LIZ, SARAH would have left with another outfitter the next morning. A Cessna Piper bound for Yellowknife had an empty seat, but she wasn't in the habit of dropping people like banana peels. She would see Liz back to the city, and from there she'd arrange for her to go home to Three Creeks. As far as the book went, Sarah no longer cared. If necessary she'd fill the space on the shelf herself. An advice book for the lovelorn. *If He Looks Like a Poet, Run!*

Flying south, they landed at two towns Mike thought they shouldn't miss. Ian asked questions and snapped pictures as if he had nothing else on his mind. Liz couldn't get enough of a church at Fort Good Hope. A little chapel on the tundra, modest and unassuming until the door opened to reveal the interior. Then, floor to ceiling, it glowed with murals. Natural dyes, Mike told them. Sarah admired the paintings from a distance, avoiding the other three.

Avoiding Liz wasn't fair. The men were another matter. She didn't want to look at Ian; didn't want to hear his voice, so calm, so interested as they toured the historic hamlet. Mike, well, Mike was an overgrown boy. That was a species she'd had her fill of during her second marriage. Why weren't there men like her father anymore? Sensible and kind. Reliable.

One more night in the Barren Lands, Mike had decreed. One more campfire, one more layer of dirt on her aching body. One more day before she could head home and forget she'd ever thought a trip like this could be fun.

THE NEXT MORNING SARAH woke up with a rock pressing into the small of her back. *Don't grump,* she told herself. *Go out there smiling.* Frontier girl. That's the story. Finish the trip on a high note. By lunch she'd be in the tub at her hotel. She would stay there for days. Until the water evaporated.

Liz was already up. Sarah didn't hear voices, though. Didn't smell coffee, either. Mike always had the coffee on early.

No coffee. No fire. No plane. She turned in a slow circle, looking in every direction. There was only one other tent. Ian's tent.

She walked past the ashes of last night's fire,

feeling the need for a better view. It didn't make any difference because they'd camped in an area without hills or eskers. All she saw was miles of nothing at all.

It was the quietest, emptiest spot Sarah had ever stood in. This must be how ants felt in the big wide world…no, because they sensed the other ants, smelled them, or had some kind of silent communication. If humans could do that, Ian would be out of his tent and beside her by now, telling her not to worry.

Maybe he did sense her fear, and wasn't coming.

Or, and this was a more appealing idea, he didn't sense her need for him because she *didn't* need him. She'd made hundreds of campfires at the cottage growing up. She could certainly brew a pot of coffee without any help from him. By the time she was done, Mike and Liz would be back from wherever they'd gone.

Happier, she found the remaining logs from the deadwood Mike had cut, and soon had the coffeepot gurgling over the flames. There was still no sign of the airplane, not so much as the drone of an engine in the distance.

"Coffee's on," she called. "Wake up, lazy-bones!"

No answer. Ian couldn't be gone, too. What

had they all done, flown off to look at a water-fall or something and left her here? They wouldn't, would they? She hadn't been that grumpy.

What if she had been, though? Grumpy enough to be left behind? Was a guide allowed to leave a woman alone in the middle of nowhere? Mike would lose his license if he did that, wouldn't he? If he had one. And Liz, darn her, would lose her contract. If she cared. Ian wouldn't lose anything. Not even a minute's peace.

She went to his tent. At least, unlike Mike's, it was still up. That was promising. She spoke through the closed flap. "Ian? Are you there? Are you awake?"

This time she heard a sleepy, questioning rumble. She couldn't believe how happy it made her. He hadn't left her alone. When he crawled out she was going to hug him and tell him how sorry she was to have misjudged him.

The zipper went up and Ian's head emerged, level with her knees. He twisted it so he could squint up at her. "What?"

Any inclination to sing his praises disappeared. "Good morning," she said.

He sat on his heels, rubbed his face and made various waking-up noises. Somehow he still managed to be attractive. Maybe it was the stubble. She was a sucker for stubble. "Well, it's the last one, so I guess that makes it a good one."

"Absolutely. And tomorrow, waking up on my million coil hotel bed, will be the best morning yet. Until then, we have a mystery."

She pointed to where the rest of the camp should be. Following her finger, Ian peered, one eye shut tight against the sun, the other squinting. No sudden alarm came into his body. Either he didn't realize what he was looking at or he wasn't surprised.

"They aren't here," she told him. "Mike and Liz and the plane. Were they going somewhere today, just the two of them? Did Mike tell you?"

Ian stood, yawning and stretching. "What do you mean, not here?" He turned, checking in every direction, as she had, still yawning, not at all concerned as far as Sarah could tell. One particularly long stretch became a bout of head scratching and ended with a wet-sounding sniff. Lovely.

"That's odd." He ducked back into his tent, then reappeared wearing his boots and a jacket. "Chilly morning. At least Mike made coffee before he left."

"Mike didn't make coffee. I made coffee. And the fire."

"You should have called me. I would have helped. You want breakfast?" He went to the trees where the food was suspended and lowered the containers to get ingredients and cooking gear. "There's a note in the frying pan."

"In the frying pan?"

"It starts with an apology. That doesn't sound good." He turned the paper over and looked at the end of the message. "There's no signature, so I don't know who's sorry."

Sarah joined him under the trees. "That's Liz's handwriting."

"'We've decided to take the plunge,' she says."

"The plunge? They've eloped? Liz is already married."

Ian didn't even smile. "Presumably there are other plunges, Sarah, besides out of one marriage and into another." He resumed reading, his voice getting harder as he went.

"'Everybody else sees that you two have things to work out but all you do is flash these "Oh, love me please, don't you dare love me" looks at each other.'"

"What?" Sarah almost squeaked the word. *Love me please, don't dare love me?* She couldn't look at Ian. "Okay, she's postpartum nuts."

"Don't be rude, Sarah."

"I'm rude? I didn't write the note." She grabbed it from him, skimmed as far as he'd got, to confirm he hadn't made it up, then continued reading silently.

"What else does it say, Sarah?"

"You won't believe it." She gave the note back to him and he read the rest out loud.

"'Sit down. Speak. Listen. Resolve. That is our gift to you.'"

"Gift!" Sarah paced away.

"After 'gift,' she's drawn one of those wink symbols people use in e-mails. An attempt, I suppose, to acknowledge how ludicrous it is. Following that bit of humor, she goes on, 'Mike wants you to know the only thing you realistically have to be concerned about is bears.'"

"Oh, my God."

Ian kept reading. "'The shotgun and shells are stacked with the other supplies. There's also a flare pistol loaded with some kind of special shell that scares bears off. Wolves, too. Mike says to make sure you continue following safe camping practices. Store and cook food away from the tents—although on the whole, it might be wisest not to cook at all, because of the aroma. As you know, it attracts them.'"

Sarah didn't know how much further her

stomach could sink. It kept dropping with every word Ian read.

"'We'll come back for you in a few days. Tuesday? That should give you time to settle your differences or whatever you need to do. Mike says he's had customers pay a pretty penny to camp in the Barrens like this. So we hope you'll enjoy the experience, when all's said and done.'"

Sarah couldn't speak. Tuesday.

"There's a P.S. 'I'll give you a hint. Relationships aren't about winning.' And that's the end of it."

"Tuesday?" Sarah said. "That's a week. That moves right along from a few to several."

He was laughing. How could he laugh?

"This isn't funny, Ian."

"I've never seen you so indignant. And that's saying something."

"I've never been left in the middle of nowhere before! There are more grizzlies in the barren lands than people, do you realize that? More wolves. Probably more wolverines, too. It's like staying out all night under some bridge in downtown Vancouver. I assure you, that isn't something I choose to do."

He had begun checking their supplies. He held the shotgun in one hand and with the other counted boxes of shells. "The difference, Sarah, is that in Vancouver you don't have me."

It was an odd feeling to want to cling to him just because he knew how to put a shell into a gun. Of course, in itself, a shell in a gun was of limited use.

"Do you know how to shoot?"

He looked at her briefly and went back to his task, filling each of his pockets with a couple of shells. Of course he knew. He'd grown up in a place similar to this, a place where polar bears came into town when they were hungry.

"I mean can you shoot straight? Can you hit what you shoot at?"

"Hopefully you won't have to find out."

She put a hand on his arm. "I want a serious answer."

"Seriously, I don't know. I used to hit what I shot at, but I haven't fired a gun in years."

"So, what do we do?"

"First things first. We have breakfast."

DESPITE THE ADVICE IN the note, Ian fried bread and eggs. Sarah needed the comfort of a hot cooked meal.

He'd been dead to the world when some awareness of her voice had got through to him. Even then, he'd known she was frightened.

Her fear gave off a different kind of tension than her anger did.

Too bad he couldn't hold her and tell her they were going to be all right, that he would take care of everything. If they could get along for ten minutes he could pretend to be the guy she needed right now.

As if he knew what that was.

A poet, she'd said, days ago. A poet to protect her, to shoot rhymes at the wildlife.

"It's an adventure, anyway," he said, while he flipped the eggs and reached for two metal plates. She didn't answer. "Here we are, the two of us united against the wilderness." It seemed like the kind of thing she'd say, with a faraway expression, happy in the land of make-believe. He wished he saw that expression now, instead of her trapped, frightened one.

She gingerly accepted a plate of food, as if a bear might jump on her the instant she touched it. "Mike and Liz won't stay away. Right? They'll realize what a ridiculous idea this was."

"Think so?" He suspected Mike had his own reasons for stranding them and wouldn't be in any hurry to come back.

"As soon as they land, as soon as they get out of the plane, I'll tackle Liz and you take Mike, okay?"

It sounded good to him. "We'll tie them up and then we'll lecture them."

"Till they beg for mercy."

He was glad to see her bouncing back. She never stayed discouraged for long.

"Can you believe them?" she was saying, soaking the last of her bread in egg yolk. "Why would Liz think it's okay to fiddle with our lives like this?"

"You've been fiddling with hers."

"That's different. What I was doing wasn't fiddling, anyway. It was encouraging her to find herself again, in the piles of diapers. To find her creative self."

"Sarah the Muse."

It was an offhand remark, but it made her sparkle. "Are you saying I have an inspiring nature, Ian?" Her voice was soft and sexy, teasingly so, but it still made him gulp. "Do I inspire you?"

"Nope."

"Bring out the best in you, then?"

"Not usually."

"No," she said regretfully, "it's the other way around, isn't it? I bring out the worst in you. I'm the Anti-Muse." She set her plate on a rock and came closer, her eyes never leaving his.

"We need to do these dishes right away," he said. "Bears, remember?"

"I thought you said not to worry about bears."

"Within reason."

She stopped inches from him, her head to one side. "Reason. Don't you ever want to let go of it?"

"Whenever I do, there's trouble."

"Don't you mean whenever you do, there's me?"

This wasn't only about sex, he saw suddenly. There was something uncertain, vulnerable, about the way she was holding herself. She needed to be wanted. Was this new, or had he been too dense to notice it before?

"Sarah."

"Hmm?"

"Bears."

She whirled around, nearly falling over.

He caught her and steadied her. Apologizing quickly and repeatedly, he said, "I meant, remember about the bears."

She pushed him away, hard. "Honestly! If I had a bad heart I'd be dead right now." Casting anxious looks all around, she picked up both plates and the frying pan. "Get the water boiling, then, if you're so worried."

SARAH DRIED THE DISHES and put them into the container for Ian to pull back up into the branches.

"Where do you think they went?" she asked. "To see Marie and her garnets? She wouldn't put up with this, if she knew. I don't think she would, anyway." That didn't mean much, though. Liz was the last person Sarah would have picked to strand her in the Arctic.

"They'll have gone back to Yellowknife."

"And tell people we decided to stay up here of our own free will?"

"Who'd ask?"

Eventually, Oliver and her parents. Ian's parents, the editor at the paper, waiting for his next column. "So right now, Mike's relaxing at the floatplane base and Liz is at the hotel having a bath?"

"And eating butter tarts."

"No," Sarah said firmly. "They wouldn't be so heartless. One look at comfy beds and restaurants and they'll turn around. I'll bet they're on their way." She shook the kettle, testing the amount of water inside. "Tea? We might as well be comfortable while we wait."

She added more sticks to the fire and placed the pot on the grill. "This is what it would have been like during the gold rush, don't you think? People like us out in the wilds. Of course, it would have been more frightening for them, without a bush plane on its way." When the water came to a boil she poured it over tea bags in two mugs.

"Sarah, I don't know how to tell you this."

Not a promising beginning, she thought.

"I've decided to walk out of here."

"Out of…" She trailed off, unsure what he meant by "here." "Out of the camp?" Because he couldn't mean more than that. Out of the Barrens wasn't possible. Out of her life, well, the timing was really bad.

"There's a Dene community not too far away. I saw it from the plane. Southeast, maybe a two-day walk."

He'd already decided, that was clear, but her welfare was tied up with his, whether he liked it or not, and she wasn't planning on leaving the relative safety of this trip wire–encircled camp. "I'm not going on any two-day walk and you're not leaving me alone."

He pulled a map from his pocket and unfolded it. "We're here." He pointed to a meaningless spot in a wide expanse. "The village is about there." He held his thumb to the mileage key, then to the space between *here* and *there*. "Fifty miles?"

Sarah's apartment was a mile from the Fraser

Press offices. She sometimes walked home—
not to work, because she didn't want to arrive
sweaty. A mile was plenty.

"I don't know if leaving the camp is a good
idea. My mother always told me if I got separated from her to stay where I was and she'd find
me. What if Mike and Liz come back?"

"They'd see us from the air."

It was unusual to feel like the careful, patient
one. For the first time Sarah had some sympathy
for the position Ian had so often occupied. Being
pulled along unwillingly by a determined, stub-
born person was uncomfortable. She wanted to
dig her heels in and make him stop.

"Mike picked a safe place to camp. What if
we walk into trouble? Animals or bog?"

"You want to wait?" He sounded as if waiting
would drive him nuts. She tried not to take it
personally.

Really, she understood his desire to take
action. Sitting passively where Mike and Liz
had left them wasn't all that palatable. "Here,
we have the trip wire, the gun, the supplies…"

"And Mike has his own agenda."

"Besides playing Cupid?"

"This has nothing to do with Cupid, not for
him."

Sarah waited, curious, but that was all Ian

said. "You're being mysterious. Did something happen?"

"I don't know for sure."

"You sounded sure a second ago. I'm not traipsing all over the place unless you tell me what you're thinking."

"I'm thinking he's made a serious error in judgment. When Marie called, so excited about the indicator minerals, that's when I got suspicious. I wanted to give him the benefit of the doubt. Who isn't tempted to do the wrong thing sometimes? I hoped he'd reconsider."

"Reconsider what, Ian?"

"The last night at Marie's camp, I think he got up to some trouble. I think he might have seeded the indicator minerals she found."

"Seeded?"

"It's an old trick. A person takes a handful of the mineral in question—gold ore, microdiamonds, garnets— and scatters them in an area to be sampled. It inflates the value of the site."

"Mike, though?" She couldn't believe he'd do something so underhanded.

"I followed him outside the area where we'd been helping Marie. He said he was working, but he didn't have tools with him. He was startled when I turned up, but at the time I thought it was because it was night and he hadn't seen me coming."

"That's all supposition, Ian."

"I know."

"Marie wouldn't be involved."

"I don't think she would, either. I think it's Mike, going outside the lines, eager to get some payoff for Marie so they can be together more than part time."

"It's really very romantic."

"Romantic? Sarah—"

"Going to such lengths for love? Taking a risk like that to be with the woman he adores?"

"Sarah."

"Marie will kill him, though. Oh, poor Marie. This will break her heart. And even if everyone knows she wasn't involved, it'll still hurt her reputation."

Ian looked relieved that her appreciation for Mike's larcenous impulses didn't go too far. "If my conclusions are right, Mike must be aware I could have seen something that night. We've been tense around each other since then. Watchful. I think he wants time to line up buyers before I can do anything to stop him. You see why I don't want to wait."

CHAPTER EIGHTEEN

THEY TOOK AS MUCH GEAR as would fit in two large backpacks. Tinned and dry food, mosquito repellent and basic first aid supplies, flashlights, two enameled mugs, two plates and a pot for boiling water and cooking. Ian hauled one of the tents and, since they couldn't be sure of finding firewood, the single-burner camp stove, as well. It didn't need much fuel. He said one small container would do. They each tied a rolled-up sleeping bag to the top of their packs.

Twenty-five miles a day. Sarah wasn't sure she'd walked that far in her entire life, let alone in one day.

Before they left camp Ian showed her how to load and fire the shotgun and flare pistol. The guns frightened her. They felt foreign in her hands, cold and unnatural. She pulled the triggers, but couldn't hold either weapon steady. If he expected her to hit anything, they were in trouble.

Every half hour they rested for five minutes,

taking a few sips of water each time. At noon and midafternoon they ate a granola bar or a handful of dried fruit.

At first Sarah kept her eyes on the ground, looking for animal tracks and overturned stones that might indicate a bear searching for ants, but gradually she relaxed. Her muscles and feet began to be her biggest problems.

Ian didn't seem to tire. He walked at an even pace, and Sarah got the impression he could go all day and night until he reached the settlement he'd seen. She distracted herself by watching the way his feet dug into the ground and the way his body leaned under the weight he carried.

After six hours she was lagging so far behind that Ian decided to stop for the day. When she caught up to him, she sank onto a boulder. Resting her muscles and feet was a huge relief, but as soon as she was stationary, flies began circling her head in earnest. No-see-ums descended in clouds. She rolled down the bug netting.

"I guess we won't be doing twenty-five miles," Ian said.

"I'm sorry."

"You're doing great. It was wishful thinking on my part."

"We'll need more than two days, then." They

hadn't brought enough food for much longer than that. "Will you still be able to reach Mike in time? Should we go back?"

Ian either didn't hear the question or didn't choose to answer it. He started striding back and forth, covering a large area. At first Sarah didn't understand what he was doing. Then she realized he was checking for signs of animals, the way Mike had done from the air.

After using ropes to suspend the backpacks several feet off the ground, he set up the tent and tossed the sleeping bags inside. He drove stakes into the ground wherever it was soft enough, then unwound the trip wire and attached it in a circle around the camp.

The last thing he did was set up the stove, choosing a flat enough rock to hold it level and pouring in a small amount of fuel. When she realized he planned to make tea she hurried over to help.

"At last. Something I have enough muscles to do. You sit, now."

He didn't argue. With a groan, he lowered himself to the ground and sat with his back against the boulder she'd abandoned. While they waited for the water to boil and the tea to steep, she told him about the book she'd bought, the one with stories of early prospectors and explorers.

"That's why you were talking about the gold rush," he said.

"A lot of the prospectors were people like me, me if I were a callow nineteenth-century youth, anyway—"

Ian smiled.

"—but a six-hour hike would have been nothing for them. They negotiated mountains and muskeg all for a chance, just a chance, of finding gold in all these empty miles."

"Humans can be tough."

"Some humans. You wouldn't catch me risking my life to look for gold. I'd stay safe at home until it was smelted and melted and shaped into something pretty to buy." She was pleased when he laughed. "But they also serve, who only shop. Right?"

"You might surprise yourself."

"What's this, you're believing in me all of a sudden?"

"No…"

Sarah laughed. His denial stung, but it was funnier than it was painful.

"I only meant you're probably tougher than you think," he said. "You'd rise to any challenge that came along, the way most people do."

"Like this morning, weeping and wailing about bears?"

"You didn't weep and wail. Besides, look at you now."

"Making tea. That *is* brave." She handed him his drink. "I do feel a little better about what's happened now that I've had a chance to get used to Liz's treachery."

"You said it the other day. You don't get bogged down." On the face of it, a compliment, except his voice was cool.

"There's no point luxuriating in misery," she agreed. "It's like that night they turned the power off." Sarah smiled at the memory. "Wasn't that fun?"

"Fun? We were *hungry.* It was cold."

"That's not the way I remember it."

SUDDENLY IT WASN'T THE WAY Ian remembered it, either. Instead of the cold and his anger over unpaid bills, he remembered diving into bed under a pile of blankets, towels and coats, laughing so much he felt warmer just from that. Then…well, then, of course, they'd made love. Played Geography and Famous People and Twenty Questions, too. Made love and played games until the late payment finally went through and the power came on.

"Sarah?"

"Hmmm?"

"What happened? With your other marriages?"

She groaned. "Are you following Liz's instructions? 'Sit. Talk. Listen….'"

"*No.* No. I've been curious about it, that's all."

"Remember what you made me promise? No touchy-feeliness during this trip."

"And I'll hold you to that. I'm wondering about facts. Not feelings."

"If I couldn't figure out what happened with Derek and Jared while sharing wine and brandy and making a complete fool of myself, I certainly can't think of anything useful to tell you now."

He didn't like hearing their names.

"I know it's weird," she said, "beginning and ending three marriages in such a short time. A rare level of failure."

"Were you unfaithful?"

"Of course not!"

"Were they?"

"I doubt it. I mean, why would they be?"

He laughed. "At least your rare level of failure hasn't dented your confidence."

"You didn't get married again, Ian? Not even once, not even for a while?"

He shook his head, partly in answer and partly in disbelief. She had a very odd way of looking at marriage. Had she ever caught the gist of the vows she'd said? The selectivity, the time frame?

"And what about us?" she asked. "You said… it was hard to live with me." She managed to smile. "It couldn't have been that bad. Not as hard as walking on your hands. Not as hard as drinking water upside down."

Again, he saw the vulnerability he'd never noticed when they were together.

"We were too different."

"Is that what happened?"

"You know what happened."

"I know what you think happened. I kept telling you it didn't."

"We were too different," he said again. "That was the main thing. Incompatible world views."

"I don't remember us being so incompatible."

"You argue all the time."

"Because you do."

"I do?"

"Even when you're wrong. Especially when you're wrong." She waved a finger at him. "That's what was incompatible with our world views. Yours were so very, very wrong."

Annoyed and amused at the same time, Ian gave up and went to heat water so they could wash before sleeping. He waited until she'd gone into the tent for the night, then shouldered the shotgun and went to collect deadwood from a fallen tree he'd seen while checking the site.

She was in rough shape already. For her, it would have been better not to leave the camp. He wasn't going back, though. Another day like this, and nothing to show for it? Sit in the shade and wait for Mike?

No way.

———

CHAPTER NINETEEN

"UP AND AT 'EM!"

Something whacked Sarah's bottom. She turned with a growl and found Ian leaning over her, holding a mug.

"*Coffee.* You angel. I was dreaming of coffee."

"No wonder—I've been waving it under your nose for about a year. Come on, get that into you and let's go. I want to make tracks today."

With every muscle creaking, Sarah crawled out of the sleeping bag and out of the tent. "I hurt."

"I know, sweetheart."

The word got her attention and she forgot to list all her aches and pains. He didn't seem to realize he'd said it. There was nothing sweet about his expression. He was focused, ready to go.

He held out an open box of crackers. "Get some of those into you. They'll help."

She took one and dunked it in her coffee.

"What was that constant racket last night? Your watch was always beeping. Didn't you notice?"

Ian shot her an exasperated look. "So sorry, m'lady. Thought you might prefer the bears being kept away."

"Are you kidding?"

"No bears came, if that's what you mean. I got up every couple of hours to feed the fire. Don't know if it helped or if there just weren't any."

Her heartbeat returned to normal. "Can we make a pact not to use the word *bear?* How about a more generic term?"

"Creatures with claws and teeth?"

"Even more generic. Like *animals* or *camp safety.*" She thought about her two suggestions. "Camp safety. Let's use that term."

"As in, so sorry, m'lady, thought you might prefer camp safety?"

"Beautiful."

SARAH MIGHT BE ABLE TO handle a twelve-mile hike, Ian thought. That put the settlement he'd seen four days away, if his estimate was right. They could at least alert Marie to what he suspected was happening. And he could contact the *Globe.*

"Did you notice," Sarah said, "that you ask

most of the questions? I hardly know anything about you. Not even where you live."

"Everywhere and nowhere."

"Very mysterious." She walked into him on purpose.

"Seriously," he said. "I share an apartment in Toronto, but I'm not there much. I'm always on the road."

"Share?" After a few minutes she asked, "With?"

"The other person who lives there."

She didn't say anything. It was one of those loaded silences. Good. Let her stew over it for a while.

He'd told her the first evening there was no one who'd mind if they slept together. Did she think he'd lied to her? Or that he had some kind of on-again, off-again thing, or an open arrangement? She'd have to know he'd never go for that.

"So it's not a relationship," she said.

"Of course it's a relationship."

"Not someone you're in love with, I mean."

"I care for her very deeply. Does that bother you?"

"Not at all."

Right. If she kept marching along like that, she'd be able to do the twenty-five miles.

"What's all this pushing and pulling, Sarah?"

"Pushing and pulling?"

She must know what he meant. She'd been doing it since she'd arrived. It was like she didn't want him, but couldn't let go of him, either.

"You're the one pushing and pulling," she said. "You always did that."

Always? How did a mildly phrased question about her behavior turn into something *he* always did?

There was no point talking to her. She'd argue whatever he said.

WHAT A HYPOCRITE! Skeptical of her, was he, when all the time he was living with some woman? *Cared very much.* Poor thing, she probably thought they had a lot more than that going for them.

Sarah reminded herself she didn't care who Ian saw. His love life had long ago stopped having anything to do with her.

She understood why the news had got to her. They were living so close together, and she was scared and hungry and more dependent on him than she liked. Once they reached the settlement, all of that would go away. She could wave goodbye without a single pang. Send his roommate flowers.

Hiking wasn't going to be the only challenge

over the next few days. The way she and Ian behaved together wore her out. She didn't use to mind conflict. Maybe she'd even liked it. From the beginning, even before they'd found so many reasons to disagree and get annoyed, being with him had made her feel as if she was teetering on the edge of something. Ready to fall, or ready to fly.

She stopped walking, slid her backpack off and took out two granola bars. "Nuts or raisins?"

"Doesn't matter." He scrunched up the wrapper and added it to the resealable bag of garbage they were carrying with them. "How much farther do you think you can go today?"

"A complete change of subject from your flaws to my fitness level? I don't think so."

They'd been walking along the top of an esker, those raised gravel ridges left by melting glaciers. Sarah sat down to rest, her legs supported by the sloping side. Ian sat, too, a couple of yards between them.

"You did say there was no one who'd mind, that night. Not lately, you said."

He waited before answering. "There isn't. I share the apartment with my sister."

His sister.

"She would have minded if she'd known," he went on, "not that I would discuss it with her.

She didn't think very highly of you for a year or two after the split."

"That's hardly fair."

"Sisters aren't fair." He took her granola wrapper to add to the garbage bag. "Shouldn't have strung you along like that, should I?"

"No, you shouldn't."

"I don't know why you're so bent out of shape about it. You have someone at home." He said the last part as if quoting.

"That."

"That? Does he know how you talk about him? Does he know about me?"

She was too aggravated to sit chatting. She stood, grimacing as she lifted her backpack and shrugged it into place. His was so much heavier, but he put it on as easily as a shirt.

"I hadn't got to the end of the sentence, Ian. That day at lunch. Someone at home, I said, and you jumped all the way to the conclusion I was sleeping around. I don't sleep around."

"Maybe we define the term differently."

He kept on doing it, no matter what she said, kept on being that cool judge. What gave him the right?

"A series of lovers, yes," she said, following the esker's path again. "Really, a series of husbands, because commitment matters. Rolls in the hay are not what I do. If you think otherwise, you don't know me."

She wished she could walk faster than he could. Leave him in the dust. Find that Dene settlement by herself. Find it first.

But no, she had to trudge behind him, unless he forced himself to match her speed. He was doing that now, which meant their elbows kept touching.

"When you wore that huge ring," he said, "I thought you'd got engaged overnight."

"I'm getting old, Ian. I can't switch allegiances quite that fast anymore."

"But there is someone."

"There isn't. There could have been. That's all I was saying."

He continued walking beside her, not giving her any idea what he was thinking. She had got caught up in defending herself and hadn't noticed until now that he was unreasonably bent out of shape, too.

A FEW MILES PAST THE POINT that had felt like her limit Ian decided to stop. Sarah could hardly move her shoulders to get her backpack off. She let it slide to the ground, then sat beside it and closed her eyes.

"Are you going to be okay?" Ian asked.

"I just need a minute."

She rested while he set up camp, then she opened a can of beans, which they ate cold, followed by a can of fruit cocktail. They used the stove to boil water, first to wash the dishes, then for tea and finally, to wash their faces and hands.

Sitting on the ground outside the tent, she drew her knees up and wrapped her arms around them. "It's colder this evening. Can we have a fire?"

"There isn't much wood here. We'd better wait." He went inside the tent and brought out a sleeping bag to wrap around her. "Better?"

"Thanks."

He'd unfolded his map and spread it out in front of them. "We've only gone half the distance I'd hoped we could cover by now. With the rations we've been taking, the food will last, just. I don't know about your feet."

"They're okay. I wish I could go faster. I don't like being out of touch with home for so long. My dad had a bit of a scare with his health. Not that I could do anything by phoning, but—"

"What happened?"

Telling him would be like giving him ammunition. "It was my fault. I mean, his doctor had told him all the things he shouldn't do, shouldn't enjoy, so it wasn't all because of me."

"What wasn't?"

"Sort of a heart attack. Not really, but close enough. Pain, an irregular heartbeat, insufficient blood flow. He lost consciousness."

"Sounds bad."

She nodded, frightened again thinking about it. Until that day, her father had seemed invincible. "It was brought on by the storm, the one that wrecked the house. More directly, it was brought on by me."

Ian raised his eyebrow. "How'd you manage that?"

"I was trying to be helpful—"

His smile was affectionate. The warmth of that encouraged her. "They were nice about it, but I knew what as on their minds because they'd said it before. 'Think, Sarah. Think before you jump.'"

He was nodding.

"You don't have to agree so easily."

"You do say 'whoops' a lot."

Sarah pulled the sleeping bag tighter. It was true, she did. Ideas seemed so good when they first occurred to her, so bright and promising, so worth grabbing. "You'd think I'd learn."

"You still haven't said what happened."

"It was a plow wind. Have you heard of those?"

"Sure. Very powerful."

"As powerful as tornadoes, but they go in a straight line instead of rotating. It pretty much left the house in pieces. The yard, too. David and Sam and I ended up in the river, along with half the trees that used to line the banks."

"You were all swept into the river?"

"Not exactly swept." She wasn't about to tell him she'd fallen in and had to be rescued. "We got in and then we got out."

"You got into the Red River, along with the microbes—"

"And the storm debris."

"One of those height-of-the-storm dips people like to take."

"Exactly." Except people were screaming and she'd thought she was going to die. Not that she'd mention that, either. "Sam had been fixing an old canoe, one we all used when we were kids."

"Not the same one you and I took on the river?"

"That's the one. He said I'd left it out in the weather. I suppose I did. He had it up on two sawhorses so he could varnish it. He'd put about a million coats on it. That canoe was never going to get another hole in it if he could help it.

"The storm had let up and we were outside checking the damage in the yard. The river had risen and the canoe had blown off the sawhorses. It began to float away. So I grabbed for it—"

"Oh, Sarah."

Something in his voice made tears come to her eyes. "I fell in and David and Sam jumped in to get me. Dad came after us with the neighbor's boat. Pulled us in."

Ian drew the sleeping bag more tightly around her, tucking it closer, and the next thing she knew his lips were against her forehead. "Sarah." It was a whisper. "When I think what could have happened…"

An all over, deep-down humming began, a murmur of feeling inside and out. She kept still, hoping he wouldn't move away.

Of course, he did. "Your dad's okay now?"

"As okay as anyone can be without bacon and coffee. Mom watches him like a hawk. I can't imagine her without him, Ian. They're like a matched set."

"My parents, too."

"How do they do it? We lasted two years."

"I guess they were meant for each other."

The humming stopped with a bang.

What had she done? Jumped into a plane to see the North, the North with Ian in it. Jumped into bed with him. Jumped into this adventure. Now here she was, alone in the wilderness with a man she'd forgotten could hurt her so easily.

She couldn't change much about the situation, but she could try for some independence. When she saw Ian collecting deadwood for the night's fire, she put out her hand for his watch. "I'll take care of the fire tonight. Out here so the alarm doesn't disturb you."

"You'd be scared."

"True. But I can feed a fire even if I'm scared."

He hesitated. "Not all night, though, Sarah. Even if you'd relieve me once so I can get a four-hour block of sleep, that'd be great. All right? You check the fire two hours from now, then come inside to sleep so I'll hear the alarm the next time."

She agreed, but only so he'd go into the tent without arguing. He'd guarded the flames for one whole night, so she would, too.

When she was alone she made sure every section of the trip wire was still fastened. It wasn't exactly imposing. A hungry or territorial wolf could easily jump over it. And how big were grizzlies, anyway? Seven feet tall? More? Wouldn't they dash the wire out of their way with one swat of a great big paw? How much would the resulting jingle of warning bells really help?

None of that pessimistic talk, she told herself. She felt for the flare gun, tucked in her waistband. It was mildly reassuring. The loaded shotgun leaned against a rock.

The quiet was something else. She almost thought she could hear Ian's heart beating on the other side of the nylon. How did people who lived up here cope? How did Marie stand it? Sarah felt irrelevant, a speck.

She half dozed by the fire, waking when it crackled, as well as when the alarm went off. Sometime during the night, Ian staggered out of the tent, walking as if still asleep.

"You didn't wake me up." He put his hand out for the watch. "My turn."

He swayed where he stood. She turned him around and pointed him at the tent. He mumbled that he'd lie down for a little longer. Ten minutes, he said. She waited until he was inside, then zipped the tent and turned back to the fire.

CHAPTER TWENTY

IN THE MORNING SARAH handed Ian his watch, then an individual-size box of cereal and a bowl of tinned oranges. When he thanked her for letting him sleep, she just smiled. The embers of the campfire were still warm. She must have kept it going all night.

"What's our target?" she asked. "Five miles? A hundred?"

"What if we don't count them? Go for thirty minute spurts until we decide to stop for the day."

"Worth a try. Maybe a planeful of caribou hunters will see us, the way Mike saw Marie five years ago. We could stop figuring out how to survive and start deciding which restaurant to go to for dinner."

"The Lair, for sure."

"I don't think so."

"It's Friday. The Bombers are playing the Lions. That was my plan for tonight. Cheeseburger and fries in front of their biggest screen."

"That's the perfect evening, is it? You look downhearted about missing it."

"The Bombers," he repeated. He knew it wasn't as much of an explanation for her as it was for him.

"I'll bet you can download the game when we reach town."

"Maybe."

"They'll play again."

He laughed at that. "Spoken by a true sports fan."

She jumped up, knocking over her cereal box. "Who do you want to be?"

"Be?"

"Winnipeg or B.C.?"

He smiled faintly. "Winnipeg, of course."

"Great." She bent over in front of him, waggling her bottom, then put her hands through her legs to hand off an imaginary ball. "We'll both be Winnipeg, all right? Guarantees we'll win. Ready? Forty-nine, sixty-three, twenty-two, hike!"

She took off across the tundra, turning and leaping to catch an imaginary pass, then zigzagging around nonexistent blockers. Then her foot slid on loose gravel. She fell to the ground and lay still.

His heart hit his boots, but when he reached her she rolled over, grinning up at him.

"Touchdown! Seven points, Winnipeg."

"Six. We still have to kick a field goal."

"Seven. Bonus point. I landed on a rock." She sat up, rubbing her left knee. "And that's the game. We won. Happy now?"

"Oh, yeah." He nodded, more affected by her lighthearted play than he could explain. "If only we do so well come the Grey Cup. Does your knee hurt? Can you put weight on it?"

"It's all right, only you'll have to carry me back to Yellowknife."

"No problem." He wanted to hold her. Hold her for the sweetness she sometimes showed. She was glowing, the way she did when she was happy. Like a light. A warm but distant light.

A wave of sadness swept over him. That distance, that was the problem. Part of it. They could talk, touch, make love, fight, have moments like this, but in the end nothing they did brought them closer together.

BY AFTERNOON SARAH'S KNEE could hardly bend.

Ian helped her sit down and gently felt her knee through her khakis. "Seems puffy." He tried to pull her pant leg up, but the material bunched around her joint.

"I can't really see." He pointed to the button at her waist. "You'd better let me take a closer look."

"Because of that M.D. you've got?"

"I have to do something."

"And taking my pants off seems like a good place to start? Normally, I'd agree with you…." She became aware that something had changed. Her knee was not his main concern anymore.

"Where's your backpack?"

What did he mean, where was it? She lifted a hand to touch the shoulder strap. It was here… Her fingers felt her jacket and only her jacket. She stared at him, horrified, thinking of the boxes and cans of food in her pack.

"When did you last have it? When we stopped for a drink?"

She tried to remember. After the football silliness she'd bundled up the garbage from breakfast, cleaning the ground as thoroughly as she could where she'd spilled some of her cereal. She'd put down the pack to roll her sleeping bag—Ian had offered to roll it for her, but she didn't want help. The more independent she was during their enforced togetherness, the better she felt. He'd called that they should hurry. And she'd taken too big a step, nearly fallen down from the pain in her knee, and then carried on.

Without the pack.

"All morning," she said. "I haven't had it all morning."

"Okay," he said calmly.

Her stomach in knots, she began to explain why it wasn't okay, that the food was miles in the wrong direction. Her sleeping bag, too. Her mosquito netting.

But mostly, the food.

"It's okay," he repeated. "We'll manage."

THEY MADE CAMP WHERE they were. Ian said it was a decent place to stay for a couple of days if they had to, protected from any bad weather by the esker they still followed, with a lake not far away over the ridge.

He picked leaves from the ever-present Labrador tea shrub and simmered them to make a drink for her. "It has medicinal properties. I don't know if they include decreasing swelling, but we might as well try."

She sipped the warm tea, hoping he knew what he was doing. Since she didn't immediately drop dead, she kept drinking. "I'm so sorry, Ian. About slowing you down, and about the food. I don't know how I forgot the pack. My shoulders ache whether or not I'm carrying it—"

"You were in pain and trying to hide it. That

distracted you." He picked up the shotgun and handed her the flare pistol. "For protection."

"I need protection?"

"I'm going to find something for dinner."

"With the gun?" She heard how ridiculous that sounded. Most of their food lay on the ground miles away, thanks to her. Finding more would involve a gun.

He climbed the ridge, and was out of sight immediately. He must not have gone far, because in a surprisingly short time she heard a shot. He returned dangling a rabbit.

Sarah was horrified. "The poor thing!" It looked like a rabbit Liz might draw, storybook soft, with long, storybook ears. "I can't believe you killed it." Her eyes filled with tears. "It probably has babies."

"Very likely."

"What'll happen to them?"

"With any luck, I'll get them tomorrow."

It wasn't funny. "They'll starve without her. Won't they? They'll wait and wait but she won't come home—"

"Are you a vegetarian?"

"You know I'm not—"

"Then hush."

She gestured helplessly. "Look at it. It has arms and legs. It's an actual being."

"It *was* an actual being, yes. That's why it's good for us. A virtual being wouldn't help at all."

She had begun crying in earnest. It wasn't logical. She loved a nice lamb roast rubbed with fresh rosemary. She loved Christmas goose with wild rice and raisin stuffing. But an hour ago this poor creature had been alive and hopping.

"A fox or a wolf would have got it eventually, if we hadn't, Sarah."

"It's my fault. Rushing up here without thinking. Actions have consequences. Why don't I ever pay attention to that? It's ridiculous, bouncing around like a child, saying 'oh, won't it be fun,' and next thing you know we're stranded and a rabbit is dead."

"Ever worn fur?"

Her tears streamed faster. She had. The collar of her gray winter coat. So soft, so amazingly soft and warm. "Not with a head."

"Not an actual being." He took the small body to a flat rock and pulled out a knife. He slipped the tip under the skin of the animal's belly and began to cut. "Well, I'll be making soup. You're welcome to have some."

IT WAS VERY GOOD SOUP. The next day, still camping in the same place, they had a very good ptarmigan. Eating freshly killed creatures and having little choice but to sit and think, Sarah couldn't avoid reviewing the events of the last several days.

Okay, truth, she told herself. Never mind Brent. Never mind perspective. When she'd seen Ian's column, what had her reaction been, really?

That she missed him. Wanted him, still. Pared down, she'd come north for one reason. For him.

She must have made some sort of sound at that revelation because he stopped working at his laptop and looked at her with concern. "Knee give you a twinge?"

"Something like that."

He raised his eyebrows inquiringly.

"I'm not as evolved as I thought."

"You have opposable thumbs, don't you?"

Sarah heaved a sigh. "All those women who worked so hard. First members of Parliament and first congresswomen, first CEOs and doctors. And what do I do?"

"You run a publishing company."

I follow a man, she thought. "I dropped everything, Ian."

Mildly, he said, "You're allowed a holiday."

"Now you're defending me?"

"Where are you going with this—evolution and feminism? What's the connection?"

They'd have to be celebrating their seventy-fifth anniversary before she would admit he was the only reason behind her trip. Partly because it would take her that long to believe it herself. "I'm thinking out loud, that's all. Stream of consciousness."

"You're getting bored."

She stood up, testing her knee. The swelling had started going down. She walked a few steps. Not bad. Maybe she didn't have miles in her yet, but soon. She found a new place to sit, a rock closer to where Ian worked.

"Do you think Liz is busy with her book?" she asked. "Or is she taking bubble baths every available moment?"

"She's likely gone home to Three Creeks to make jam. Are you wishing for a bubble bath?"

"I really am."

"Remember, people pay Mike big money for an experience like this."

"Silly people. Actually, it's not bad out here. If there was hot running water—"

"And wine and books."

"Movies."

"Restaurants."

"Soft mattresses and clean sheets."

"Other than that—"

"Wouldn't change a thing." She laughed.

"My needs are so basic. Take everything away and what do I care about? Hot water, in all its forms. Spraying down on me. Soaking all around me. In a teapot. Dripping through fresh ground coffee. Am I thinking about Dickens? Einstein? Plato? No. Just—"

"Hot water."

"Exactly. You can put it on my tombstone, Ian. *She loved hot water.*"

"This discovery has been a terrible shock for you."

"A real eye-opener," she agreed. "Why spend all those years in school? Why didn't I just boil water? You're proving to be a much more complex person than I am."

"I thought I was a bunny murderer."

"I can't fault you there, since I'm a bunny eater. Delicious bunny, by the way, thank you." She sent him another questioning look. "This is who you are, isn't it? You're not a city guy at all."

"I can be."

"But if you were to draw a picture of the real you, this would be it, wouldn't it?"

"Bunny killer?"

"Outdoor guy."

"Maybe."

"Cerebral outdoor guy. You keep us safe. You hunt. You write. For all I know you've started a book about this experience, or poems about the spiritual connection you feel for the land. And all I do is groan—"

"About hot water."

"You won't put me in the book, will you? Show my dorkiness to all?"

"It's a column."

"Next week's column? 'All my companion did was complain, so I heaped stones around her and turned her into an inuksuk.' No one would blame you, Ian. Just don't use my name."

THE DAY THEY'D BEEN IN Tukoyaktuk, Ian had e-mailed the column that had come out of the diamond-related interviews in town and the visit to Marie's camp. For the next one he'd wanted to focus on the Barrens, so in a way he couldn't be in a better situation.

His laptop battery hadn't drained yet. He sat on one rock and used another, flatter one, as a desk.

The size of this place, he typed, *the isolation, the potential for danger…they're hard for a city person to grasp. You have to know what you're doing to survive here. There's no corner store or pizzeria to bail you out, no easy entertainment. You have to be able to rely on the people you're with, to know who'll pull you out of the river, make you laugh, make your efforts worthwhile.*

He read the last sentence. He'd pull Sarah out of the river. He wasn't sure she'd do the same for him. *You're drowning, just like Shelley.*

He'd been content before Sarah turned up. Life in order, emotions on an even keel. For a while after she'd gone, he'd been a real mess.

It was a mystery to him that a person could be complete and then, after meeting someone, living life with someone, that self-sufficiency could disappear. When Sarah left, she'd taken a chunk of him with her.

He'd lost her family, too. Stopped having any right to visit at the welcoming, moldering house or the Whiteshell cabin.

Then she arrived with excited where've you beens and how've you been doings. She had obviously wanted a long, reacquainting heart-to-heart that proved there were no hard feelings. She wanted sex to make everything better. She still hadn't learned that no matter how great the sex was, it didn't fix the rest.

He'd pull her out of the river. She made him laugh. It would be great if that was enough.

HE HAD CHUCKLED about the inuksuk, but he hadn't reassured her that she wasn't whining or that he'd never, ever, cover her with stones. Sarah wished she could read what he'd written next.

After stretching out and closing his eyes to rest, he'd gradually fallen silent.

"Ian?"

She went closer to see if he was ignoring her, or sleeping. His face was relaxed, his breathing shallow. Rhythmic.

Poor guy. He had to be exhausted. He might as well rest. By now, she was sure it must be too late to stop Mike or warn Marie. She'd lost count of the days, but she thought it was probably Sunday. Saturday? Soon Mike would fly back for them.

He would, wouldn't he? Once a person had crossed such a definite and visible line it was hard to know which others they might choose to cross, as well. What if Mike didn't want them found? He had to be worried about what Ian might do.

Liz wouldn't forget them, though.

Sarah almost didn't mind that Liz had stranded them. With nowhere to run, she and Ian had to deal with each other. At least when they went their separate ways again it would be on better terms.

When she got home, she wouldn't call Brent, not about anything besides Jenny's health. She knew she didn't have a future with him. He'd be part of the same sad pattern—one she didn't want to follow anymore.

It was a wonderfully freeing feeling.

No more optimistic diving into dead-end relationships. She felt like cheering. Calling someone. Oliver, a girlfriend, her parents. *No more pathetic marriages, Mom!*

With very little pain, she had reached the top of the esker. On the other side was the lake where Ian had been getting their water. If only it was a hot springs lake. She could take the biodegradable soap and get clean for the first time in days. Float and soak, ease her muscles and her knee.

But it was glacier fed. If the water in Yellowknife was chilly, here it had to be downright cold. There was a time when she wouldn't have cared. Slicing through that clear blue sparkle would have seemed worth a touch of hypothermia. She blamed her hesitation on her unplanned dip in the Red River.

She looked all around. There was no sign of fauna other than the still-sleeping Ian.

This, she knew, was an example of what she did—jumped into things without thinking. But she *was* thinking. It would be cold, she would get bitten, but mostly, she would get clean.

Excited flies and mosquitoes gathered as soon as she took off her hat and jacket. She slid down the esker's side to their camp, expecting the sound of falling gravel to wake Ian. It didn't.

She got the bug spray from his pack and sprayed it all over, but these bugs weren't quitters, so she helped herself to his mosquito netting, too.

Back over the esker, this time with more twinges from her knee. The ground was marshy here, so she left her clothes on the ridge, and as quickly as she could, wrapped herself in the netting, squishing insects as she went. At the lakeshore, she unwound the mummy bandages, and without giving herself time for doubts, jumped into the water.

She gasped at the cold. A fly landed on her forehead and took a big bite. She smacked at it and it moved to the top of her head.

There was nothing else to be done.

She dived under. It was cold and clear. Amazingly cold and amazingly clear.

THE FIRST THING IAN THOUGHT when he woke up was that a bear had got into his pack. It was a horrifying moment, because Sarah was gone. Then he saw that only the netting and repellent had been disturbed.

He climbed on top of the esker to scan the area. There she was, near the lake. But what was she doing? Dancing? Slowly turning, arms out, covered in white. Completely covered, head and all.

When he got closer he saw that her hair was wet and she was shivering.

"Sarah!"

She didn't look at him, but her movements became more seductive. She had been turning all in one direction. Now she reversed, and the white cloth began to peel away.

When he reached her, he took off his jacket to wrap around her, but she twirled faster, avoiding him. Another turn, another layer unwound.

"It's the famed Dance of the One Long Hunk of Mosquito Netting, I see."

She pirouetted closer, blinking at him through the gauzy cloth. "Want to unwind me?"

Boy, did he.

The layers continued to thin. "Look at you," he said. "Definitely not the prim children's editor. More like Jezebel."

"Which do you prefer?" she asked, managing with her tone of voice to play the two roles at once.

"Can't choose." *Both. Separately and together, like this. Don't change a thing.*

"And who are you in this pantomime?" She edged closer. "The audience, bored to tears with the whole darn thing? A monk, gritting his teeth on his celibacy? Or the chivalrous knight, a gentleman no matter what the cost?"

"I'm not sure I'm in any pantomime—"

"Of course you're in it."

"Well, then, I'm the puzzled ex."

Her body tilted toward him. "I'm a puzzle? Do you spend much time trying to solve it? Days and days? Years and years?" She got closer and sparkled more with every question. "Am I never far from your thoughts?"

Like he was going to admit that. Wait until they reached some form of transportation— bush plane, dogsled or bicycle—she'd take off for Vancouver without a backward glance. This was just entertainment for her.

"It's what you said before," he told her. "You have a special place—"

She twisted to his side. "On the periphery?"

"That's right."

"Or am I everywhere?" She moved behind him. He felt her body undulate toward him, touching, not touching, touching. Then she was at his side, then in front of him. He stepped back so she couldn't press against him again.

She lifted an arm, bringing a veil of netting between them. "Do you think in another life I was a Druid priestess?"

"I think you were the boss of the Druid priestesses. If they had priestesses."

The veil came down. "Now you're saying I'm bossy?"

"I'm saying you're sublime."

She stood still, staring at him, and any hope that he hadn't said the words out loud died.

SARAH LAUGHED, TRYING TO sound genuinely amused. She didn't want him to think for a second that she'd taken that remark seriously. Rewinding the netting around her body as she went, she began circling back to her clothes.

Ian disappeared over the other side of the esker while she dressed. When she joined him, he'd started water heating on the stove and had his sleeping bag out for her to wrap herself in.

He waited to tell her off until she'd downed two cups of tea and stopped shivering. "Going in the lake was reckless."

"I disagree."

"Do I need to tell you all the ways it was dangerous?"

"I know all the ways. After due thought, I decided to go in, anyway. It was lovely. A celebration. And, of course, a bath." A cause for jubilation in itself.

"You were celebrating another day of hunger and anxiety?"

"I was celebrating my freedom." She couldn't describe the whole train of thought, because too much of it involved him. But he did look as if he needed an explanation, so she said, "I'm not getting married anymore."

"Ever?"

"Probably." Ever sounded too *final*. She didn't think her decision had gone that far.

"Your knee seems better. You're getting restless."

"I've memorized this particular part of the skyline," she agreed. "And I'm on a first name basis with most of the bugs that have bitten me. Maybe it's time we started walking again."

He looked cautious rather than pleased. "We'll try it tomorrow."

CHAPTER TWENTY-ONE

FIFTEEN MINUTES WALKING. Fifteen minutes resting. It wasn't just Sarah's knee that slowed them down. The esker that had provided a raised, dry path had curved to the east. They were picking their way across low-lying ground, trying to avoid spongy marshland. And she'd thought the bugs were bad before.

Ian had been quiet all morning. Pensive.

"Something on your mind?" she asked.

"Just thinking."

"See? This is an example. You were always like this."

"Would you stop with the always?"

"This is the pulling away part of what you do. Not to embarrass you, but yesterday you called me sublime… Now you're not even here. I used to want to knock on your head and say let me in."

"I did let you in."

"Right. You're worrying me."

"I don't mean to."

He sped up. Sarah was sure he was intentionally going faster than she could go. For a while she tried to think about books in production. Her feet were too sore to concentrate on that, so she tried thinking about food.

If she could have one dessert with her, and one only, which would it be? She narrowed it down to a few old standbys. Oatmeal-raisin cookies. Brownies. Butter tarts. Pumpkin pie.

And that took her right back to location. Where was she on the huge map of the Northwest Territories and where was the nearest bakery?

Ian had slowed down. "Doing okay?"

"I'm adding up the populations of the places we've been. Roughly, I don't remember exactly. Twenty thousand in Yellowknife, three thousand, four hundred in Inuvik, something under a thousand in Tuk, six hundred and some in Fort Good Hope—" She paused while she added in her head. "Twenty-five thousand."

"Don't forget Marie in her camp."

"And one. That leaves quite a few people who might be in the Barrens."

"Mostly along the Mackenzie and the other main rivers, I think. Except for that grouping I saw from the plane."

"Maybe it was a mirage."

They must have gone another mile before Ian spoke again. "I thought the village was close. Maybe you're right. Maybe it was a mirage. I've been thinking about that. It might have been rocks and I just thought it was a settlement because I couldn't accept so much space without people. Or it might have been a temporary camp, like Marie's."

"Could we be going in circles?"

He shook his head. "I've been keeping the setting sun on my right each evening, so we're still going south. It's hard to navigate, though, when hardly any stars are visible."

So there was some uncertainty. "Sounds like we should be fine."

They'd reached an area of higher ground, dry underfoot and scattered with rocks. Ian removed his backpack and the other gear he was carrying, and sat on a smooth, worn boulder big enough for both of them.

"I'm really sorry. I didn't want to wait for them to come back, like some idiot. Instead I'm leading you who knows where like some idiot."

She laughed. "It's not who knows where, it's southeast. Maybe the community you saw is only a quarter mile away."

"Maybe we've gone past it."

"Then maybe Yellowknife is a quarter mile away."

He smiled, but his expression remained bleak. "A person could really get lost out here. Seriously lost."

She sat next to him and leaned in, nudging him with her shoulder. "An eternity here with you wouldn't be the worst thing."

"Pretty nearly, I imagine."

"That depends. Would there be perks?"

Amusement only emphasized his fatigue. "If we were spending eternity here, sure."

"So under those circumstances, and those circumstances alone—if we wandered the spirit world of the Barren Lands forever—then you'd make love with me again?"

"It would only be fair, having lost you, to occasionally give in to your demands."

"Oh!" She flung herself against him and knocked him over. Too late to stop, she remembered the rocks all around them, but when they landed she felt his body shaking with laughter.

"You're getting ahead of yourself, Sarah. We're not dead yet." But he rolled, taking her with him, pinning her to the ground. He pulled up the netting of his bug hat, then, more slowly, pulled hers up, too. With no sign of reluctance, he kissed her, a light touch at first and then deeply.

Both at the same time, they pulled away.

"Bad plan," Sarah said.

"Yes."

"I really think we should consider giving in to this chemistry thing. Once we're home, I mean."

"You mentioned that before."

"I read that happy people are the ones who make sure they do what they enjoy." He was still close enough that she could feel him chuckle. "We could get together four times a year, each solstice and equinox. Or twelve times, the first of every month." She moved closer to him again, and kissed him lightly. "Or fifty-two times, every Monday."

"There's football on Mondays."

She didn't rise to the bait. "Football. What's happened to you, Ian? There was a time when you seduced me with beautiful quotations. 'All things…'"

"Right, that."

"Was it just a line?"

"Sarah, you weren't the sort of girl to hand lines to."

Vague, as compliments went, but she liked it. "And you read me Shakespeare's sonnets. Remember?"

"You read them."

"I believe I forced you to take a turn."

He nodded. "You wanted me to write a sonnet for you."

"And you wouldn't! You whispered something, but it wasn't a sonnet. I should have known then."

"That I wasn't a poet? Yeah, I certainly gave you a heads-up about that."

"Want to try again? Compare me to a late summer's day in the North?"

"I'm not sure you compare to summer."

"You'd better not tell me I'm in the autumn of my days."

"Not autumn, either. If you were a planet you'd revolve around the sun in one day. All the seasons, warmth, rain, storms, cold all at once."

"That makes me sound unpredictable. Erratic."

"No, it's predictable. I expect it."

"I'm not erratic," she protested. "I don't like the word."

"How about mercurial?"

Mercurial was only slightly better, but she didn't mind him saying it because he was looking at her kindly. More than kindly. "If that's true, you're the only person who makes me that way. You're the heat source."

"The sun?"

"No, no—"

"You revolve around me, do you? I'm the center of your universe?"

"Absolutely *not*. You're the virus that makes my mercury go up."

He touched her forehead. "Seems cool enough." Then her nose. "Damp. That's good, isn't it? What are your symptoms?"

His touch made her body heavy. "General malaise. Aching muscles."

"Poor thing. Where does it hurt?"

She put a hand to her stomach, hesitated, then moved it a few inches lower. "Here."

"Want me to fix it?"

"Please."

He felt under her sweater for her belt, loosened it, then flicked open the button and eased the zipper down. "Here?" he said, touching her skin.

She nodded.

He bent and kissed a spot right under her belly-button, then a spot below it and a spot below that. "Better?"

"Worse."

"Uh-oh. 'First, do no harm.'" His hands were at her hips, moving down, pulling her khakis lower, finding exactly the spot that ached to be touched.

Everywhere he went, mosquitoes did, too, but she didn't care. She wriggled to get her legs free of the constricting cloth, then pulled him between them. She heard his zipper and felt him against her, tantalizing, barely touching. Then at last he was deep inside. His strength filled her, made her his, made her feel the ground, made her part of the ground. It was a new feeling, the opposite of flight. Rooted and real.

Gradually, she became aware of twigs and biting insects. Even then, they didn't seem to matter.

"Well," she said, her voice heavy and content, "look at you. A great bear of a man." He seemed startled, as if that couldn't be a good thing, so she added, "A great, *lovely* bear of a man."

That was the end of it, though. Neither of them could relax once that word had been spoken.

"There's tundra in my hair." She ran her fingers through, pulling out coarse stems and a rust-red flower. "I should press this. In my *Complete Works of Shakespeare,* how's that?"

He picked out another bloom. "And I'll press this in mine."

CHAPTER TWENTY-TWO

SARAH WAS RIGHT. They should have stayed at Mike's camp.

"One more day," he said. "Then we'll use rocks to write a message for planes going overhead."

"Sounds good. If any do go overhead."

A question was on his mind, and although this might not be the time to ask it, he wanted to hear her answer. He handed her the water bottle, full of lake water boiled that morning. She drank only a little of it. If they were on the right path they should reach another lake by afternoon, but until they were sure of more supply they needed to conserve.

"Yesterday got me thinking."

"I didn't think at all. I smiled myself to sleep."

"I stayed awake half the night." Wondering if they could have handled their problems differently. Spent the last ten years together. "Have you ever been able to explain our marriage to yourself? Why it tanked so quickly?"

Her shoulder lifted in a long, slow shrug. "You didn't trust me."

That wasn't an explanation. It was how things were between them. The state of their union. "Our relationshiop wasn't based on trust. It was—"

"Sex."

She'd never sounded bitter about it before. "More than that. A real pull toward each other—"

"And a real push away. That's what I mean. That's the trust deficit."

He didn't see how he could have trusted her. "Why couldn't we say we were fine with each other in spite of that? Given everything else we had, all the good stuff."

"Because we weren't."

Unusually brief, for Sarah. He'd hoped for more detail.

She went on. "It's a decision, isn't it? To accept or not. Not so much Fate or Cupid's Arrow, but a conscious decision. And we decided no."

"Maybe it was the wrong decision."

"You blew up. You made all sorts of accusations and then you left."

"To take a walk."

"Some walk!"

"A long walk."

"*Nine* days."

"And when I came back you were gone."

She looked at him in surprise, real surprise. "I didn't know you went back. I would have stayed if I'd known you were coming back."

"You wouldn't have. You had your pride."

NOT REALLY, SARAH THOUGHT. She'd carried it in tatters back to her parents' house.

She ached to think of Ian going into that empty apartment. Would she have stayed? She had no idea. The missed opportunity felt like a hole in front of her, one that widened the longer she thought about it.

If she'd stayed they might have made up. Apologized and explained and made love and tried harder to understand each other.

"Nothing happened with that guy, you know. I kept telling you that. I don't even remember his name. It's like you said the other day. I can't help how men look at me."

"Sure you can."

"Oh, right." That was unfair. "Wear sack-cloth and ashes? Take a page out of your book and let them all know how very much I disapprove of them?"

He frowned. "I don't see anything wrong with disapproving of men who leer at my wife."

"Not just them. Me. You disapprove of me." For a horrible moment she thought she was going to cry. She gulped, but the tightness in her throat didn't go away. She hated it, hated it, when he looked at her and found her wanting. Less than he expected. Less than he wanted.

"Don't cry, Sarah."

"I'm not." She put a hand over her mouth to make it stop trembling.

They had forgotten to walk. They'd been standing, almost shouting at each other for she didn't know how long. No, she had been almost shouting. Ian had been talking so quietly and calmly it chilled her.

"You do flirt. You enjoy the attention."

Here it was now, the truth as he saw it. From *I don't disapprove* to all the reasons why he did.

"You were married to me and you flirted with him."

"We talked about the class we were taking. That's all."

"You went out for espresso and talked about poetry. While I was working and paying the bills."

She didn't know what to say because in fact the other student had ended one of those study sessions by suggesting they go back to his place. Ryan? That might have been his name. She'd been shocked. She'd told him off.

"We should have stuck to the library. Would that have helped?"

"Some."

"He wasn't the only problem, then."

"Of course he wasn't. He was more like a symptom of how you thought about things."

"How *I* thought?" She was getting tired of being the villain. "You were blameless, were you?"

"There's no such thing as blameless."

"He said, oh, so correctly."

"We were married, I was working."

"And that bothered you, right? Because that's what you said before, too. You said you were paying the bills. So it bothered you that I took extra classes—"

"Not that you took them—"

"That I stayed in school all summer while you worked."

"That you stayed *at* school all the bloody time. Talking bloody Shakespeare with every drooling guy who wanted to buy you coffee!"

Silence simmered between them.

"Then I guess you weren't paying for everything," she said finally. "If they wanted to buy my coffee, you weren't paying all the bills." She couldn't believe how childish she sounded, how childish she felt. But the point, as small as it was, needed to be made. He couldn't have it both ways.

"I don't want to do this, Sarah—"

"You started it."

"How ridiculous is this? We're lost in the Arctic and we're fighting."

In a small voice she said, "Subarctic."

He made a gesture of agreement, peeved agreement. "By all means, let's be accurate."

"You're the one who always wants to be accurate."

"And *that* bothers you."

"Yes, absolutely. Because the exact, accurate truth is sometimes beside the point. What someone really means, really feels—what's going on underneath the apparent facts—that's what matters."

"And that's what I tried to tell you ten years ago."

Sarah blinked, wondering what she'd got herself into.

"Preferring to stay at school," he continued, "preferring to have sandwiches at the cafeteria, preferring to stay out late when you knew I was at home. Those are the things that mattered."

"Okay." She nodded, tears once again threatening. "So I screwed up." She didn't want her voice to shake, so she waited a moment. "On the other hand, Ian, I could say that preferring to stay home fuming, preferring to get angry, preferring not to understand what was going on with me…those were choices, too. They mattered, too."

He paced a few steps away, then turned back. "You're saying I should have sucked it up? Waited for you to grow up?"

"You really think it was all my fault, don't you?"

"I suppose I do."

His coldness was the worst thing. His cold disapproval. It made her feel like a worm. She couldn't have been that bad.

They started walking again, misery hanging in the air.

THE ENERGIZING SENSE OF being in the right kept Ian going for miles. Gradually, the improbability that he'd been the one perfect thing in their marriage began to get through to him. Being blameless didn't seem very likely.

She'd been central in his life. It burned him that he hadn't mattered as much in hers. It burned that she so quickly found someone else, while he went on missing her.

Even the Serengeti safari had managed to be about her. She might as well have been there, because he'd seen it through her eyes. Pictured how she would have loved the wide-open spaces, with herds of zebra instead of cattle, and been thrilled by the lions, maybe scared, too, maybe shrinking against him to be held. How she would have wept to see the dead elephant calf, ditto with the shrinking. As if Sarah would ever shrink into anyone's arms. Shrinking wasn't her thing.

It was an odd idea, now that he thought about it. Wanting someone to shrink wasn't very nice. Did he really want her smaller and quieter, less than she was?

Maybe he did.

That was awful. Not just awful, but pointless, like pressing a flower or sticking a pin through a butterfly, and expecting them to stay as beautiful as they were while they bloomed or fluttered.

And if that was what he wanted, a smaller, quieter, pressed and pinned Sarah, he didn't really have any right taking any moral high ground, did he?

HOURS LATER, THEY STOPPED to make camp. Ian began scouting the area before setting up the tent. Her body stiff and creaking, Sarah sat down to loosen her shoes, then eased them off.

Her feet burned and, thanks to her bout of nudity the day before, she itched everywhere.

They'd hardly said a word to each other since the fight. This interlude was going to end the way it had started, with coldness and suspicion. Their lovemaking had been so intense, they'd been so emotionally exposed. How was that possible, with this anger brewing?

He wasn't her Ian anymore. Not the boy who'd been eager to fall in love and not the disillusioned husband, either. It was time to accept that. He was a stranger. A stranger who happened to know her flaws.

And she'd done that to him. She'd started the change.

Something in his posture got her attention. He stilled, then crouched to look more closely at the ground. Before he straightened, she'd stuffed her feet back into her shoes and hurried to him.

"What is it?"

"We'll have to go farther."

Her heart thudded. "Okay."

He scared her more when he handed her the flare gun. The grip fit easily in her hand. Her finger automatically curved around the trigger. He checked that both barrels of the shotgun were loaded. She'd never seen his expression so hard.

"Let's go."

"Long claws?" she asked.

"Three, four inches."

That meant grizzly.

They were walking so fast she was already breathless. "How far do we need to go?"

"I don't know."

"Miles?"

"Grizzlies have a huge range. I doubt we can walk out of this one's territory tonight. Away from recent tracks will be the best we can do."

They walked until the sun was low, then picked the safest site they could find for their tent. No nearby water, no rocks large enough to give an animal shelter, no sign of berries or ants. They took extra care setting up camp, then sat in the scant protection of the bell-rigged wire. There was no firewood to collect, so they turned on both flashlights, aiming the beams outward.

"Go into the tent and sleep, Sarah."

She stayed where she was. "I don't want to leave you."

"Going to protect me?"

She managed a quick, tired smile. "I owe you. You rescued me from the man at the café."

"That feels like years ago. I don't know what I thought I was doing."

"Warning him off."

"He wasn't my business. Was I always arrogant?"

"You were always…certain of things."

"Arrogant."

"Young and determined. Wanting to avoid mistakes." This was the first time she'd realized that.

"And yet making them all the time."

"Me, too. Ian, I don't want to be alone."

He brushed her cheek with his hand. "I know. You need to sleep, though. After the day we've had…tomorrow will be easier for you if you're rested."

It took all her courage to offer to take turns guarding, the way she had the second night out.

To her relief, he wouldn't agree. "Sleep," he said again. "I'll be here, a few feet away." A brief smile softened his expression. "And if I see any movement out there, I'll scream. Okay?"

AT FIRST, ADRENALINE KEPT Ian alert, but as the night wore on fatigue took over. Afraid of drifting off and leaving Sarah unprotected, he stayed on his feet and paced from one end of the wired encampment to the other.

"Ian?" He heard the tent zipper, then the

scrambling noises of Sarah coming outside. "Thought I'd talk before I moved. Didn't want to scare you, or get shot."

"Can't sleep?"

"Why don't you try? I can look like a terrifying human as well as you can."

The offer touched him. He wouldn't ask her to do that, though. He'd put her through enough already, insisting on this debacle of a hike.

"I want to tell you something, Sarah." He felt her stiffen. Only went to show how often he said anything she wanted to hear. "Just that I know it takes two to wreck a marriage." Seeing how much her body relaxed made him wish he'd admitted it much sooner.

"I suppose we did the best we could," she said. "Our parents told us we were too young."

"I refuse to believe that first year was a mistake."

"The first year was great."

"Maybe we should remember to appreciate that."

IT WAS HARDLY MORNING when they got on their way. Sarah's knee hadn't responded well to yesterday's pace. She hated being the one to limit what they could do.

No matter how frightened a person was, it

was difficult to stay on high alert for long. The day began to feel like any other. Walk southeast, rest, drink, snack, walk.

It made a difference to her that Ian had accepted some responsibility for how their marriage ended. Even though it had been really unpleasant when they did it, she was glad they'd hashed things out. They weren't as brittle with each other now. A definite sadness had taken over, though, where tension and anger left off.

"I liked what you said about being fine with each other. That's what I used to wish, that you'd be more like Mr. Rogers." Too late, she saw she was still doing it. Not being fine with him.

He didn't call her on it. "Never watched the show. We didn't get many channels when I was a kid."

"He had a song about people liking each other just the way they were. I wished you felt that way. Liked me for better or worse."

"I did. Finding fault isn't the same as not liking. Not that I should have found fault—" He froze. "Sarah. Listen to me."

"I have been listening. I've heard everything you've said these past few days—"

With one hand he took the pistol from her waistband and cocked the hammer, with the other he pushed her behind him. "Don't run."

Hardly breathing, she looked over his shoulder. At a bear. A huge, bristling bear.

Everything in her wanted to run. Run for the hills. Except there weren't any hills. No doors to shut. No locks to turn. There was only Ian.

The animal stood up on its hind legs. Towering. Swaying. Sniffing the air.

"He's checking us out," Ian said softly. "Figuring out what kind of creatures we are. Back away, Sarah. Slowly. Keep backing away."

She did as he said, feeling in her pocket, past her lip gloss, to the atomizer of bear spray. She got it out and flicked off the lid. It was a very little thing to hold in her hands.

Her fear zoomed into high gear when the bear dropped back down on all four feet. It snapped its jaws together and made a dog-like sound, part woof, part growl. Sarah's legs could hardly hold her up.

"Keeping going, sweetheart. It's trying to scare us."

"Oh. It's doing such a good job."

And then it charged.

Everything happened at once. Sarah pointed the bear spray, with her hand shaking too much to aim the nozzle or activate the can, and then her legs gave way beneath her. Ian fired the pistol. A loud, bright flash went off and the bear veered to the side. She smelled it as it went past.

Ian handed her the pistol. "Load it." He turned in the direction the bear had gone, shotgun ready. They waited, Ian with the gun and Sarah shivering, but it didn't come back. Not then.

CHAPTER TWENTY-THREE

IAN WAS WORRIED ABOUT SARAH. Over and over, she had apologized for not being able to reload the flare pistol. Her mind had gone blank, she said. She couldn't remember where to find the flares, or how to put them in the gun.

So he'd shown her again what to do, and made her repeat the actions several times, reciting the steps as she went. He wanted them etched in her mind. The pistol was tucked in her waistband now, along with an extra flare.

Finally, the landscape was showing signs of change. More trees, still only dotted here and there, but it meant he and Sarah were going the right way, toward the boreal forest south of the tundra. It also meant they had something to burn, something to shelter in, something to climb. Barren land grizzlies weren't big fans of forest. The boundaries of the bear's territory had to be close. Soon, things would get better.

The next time they came to an area with a

few trees and no signs of animal tracks or scat or scavenging, he put down his backpack, leaned the gun against some rocks and began to put up the trip wire. If Sarah didn't take a nap soon, she was going to drop. He wanted to set up the stove and boil water for tea. The warmth would be good for her.

"Ian."

"Just a second." He was having trouble securing the stakes for one corner of the trip wire.

She said his name again, louder. He looked up and saw her pointing the flare gun at him.

Not at him. Her eyes were focused behind him.

He turned in time to see the grizzly walking purposefully his way.

HER FINGERS WERE LIKE WOOD. She found the trigger. If it was the wrong thing to do, if she only made the bear angry...

She aimed above and to the side of the creature, and fired.

There was a burst of light and a whistling explosion. The animal paused. Only paused.

Ian dived and rolled to the shotgun, grabbed it, pointed it. But he didn't fire.

"Ian?" She fumbled for the second flare, loaded it. The bear was nearly on him. What if she hit Ian?

Above the grizzly. Anywhere above it.

Another light, another roaring noise.

The bear moved its head from side to side. It looked mildly annoyed. It refocused on Ian.

Sarah ran to the backpack for another flare. Loading it as she went, she started toward the animal. She saw the long barrel of the shotgun nearly touching its neck. That was when Ian fired. And fired again.

IAN PULLED SARAH TO HIM and told her how amazing she was. He kissed her forehead and her tear-streaked face and held her tight. They were both shaking.

The bear sprawled beside them. Sarah stared at it with a mix of horror and pity. "Why did you wait so long? I nearly died, watching that bear get so close."

"Bears aren't easy to stop. You have to wait for the right shot." He touched her chin, her cheek, feeling her softness, thinking how close he'd come to leading her into disaster. He kissed her again, ashamed to find his lips were trembling.

"Shh," she said. "It's all right. We're all right. Your lips feel lovely. You should always kiss me."

"Deal."

"Let's go home."

Slowly, not quite in control of their wobbly arms and legs, they reorganized their gear, located south-east and started walking again.

"Remember *Jaws?*" Sarah asked. "The shark spouse, how vengeful it was? What if bears are like that?"

"They aren't. Mothers with cubs, look out. Males and females couldn't care less about each other. Geese now, they're another matter. They mate for life. Robins, could be fierce, too."

"Poor thing."

He might be in one piece physically, but he felt strange. Woozy. Punch drunk. Flight-or-fight hormones, maybe, plus the effects of so little sleep.

When the bear had charged that first time it likely would have veered even if he hadn't used the pistol. There were lots of stories about that kind of behavior. The threatening posture and noises, followed by the headlong charge. It was meant to terrify and it did. Often, that would be enough of a defense. A fight was always a risk; most animals would rather avoid one.

But this bear had taken a good look at them and come back. Its calm, quiet approach the second time was hunting behavior. If not for

Sarah, Ian had no doubt it would have killed him before he could reach the shotgun.

"Sarah, did I thank you?"

"For what?"

"The flares, woman."

She managed a smile. "Oh, that. Yes, you thanked me."

He could hardly reconcile her today with the woman who'd walked into the bar in her sexy business suit, or with the girl he'd met all those years ago. Long, straightened hair, jeans and a Guess Who T-shirt, excited to be on campus. He hadn't let himself think about her, not for a long time.

First day of classes he'd noticed her and thought, *Wow, she's hot.*

But she was complicated, and hard to read. Especially since the only girls he'd known up to that point were ones he'd grown up with, played with since kindergarten.

Sarah was different. Always on the verge of laughter. Teasing. Growing into her sexuality and enjoying the power.

"You're a very smart boy, aren't you," she'd said after class one day—statement, not question—and he'd right away been annoyed with her.

Boy. Not what a guy wanted to hear at

eighteen when he was new to the city. Was she making fun of him? He'd had no idea what to say to her. *Oh, yeah?* Not an effective retort.

So he'd made do with a cold, hard stare, thinking *Bond, James Bond* (Brosnan at the time), and the sparkle in her eyes had turned to a slow burn.

"Come get a cup of coffee with me." It had sounded like a command. He was tempted to blow her off on principle, but he really wanted to go with her.

They went to a coffee shop on Portage Avenue, across from the university. To him, then, this was big-time sophistication. She'd ordered espresso as if she'd been drinking it every day of her life, so he did, too, cup after cup at a buck ninety-five a shot. He had to walk everywhere for the next two weeks, completely out of bus money. They talked on and on while the sun went down, discussing Middle English poetry the whole time. The more she analyzed iambic pentameter, the more he wanted to kiss her. He never drank espresso again without thinking of her lips.

Her voice jogged him back to the present.

"Maybe if we were spies, or forest rangers, we'd do better together," she said. "Because with sex or emergencies, we're good. If we could live in a constant state of arousal, in one form or another, we'd be okay."

He thought about telling her they might be okay anyway, okay with a lawn to mow and a driveway to shovel. Couldn't push that, though. Not if she still needed some kind of romantic haze in her life.

"Sar? Look. Over there." He pointed.

He could hardly believe what he was seeing, but Sarah seemed to see it, too. No mirage. Real.

Several all-terrain vehicles and a group of men. Waving.

CHAPTER TWENTY-FOUR

THE STEADY HUM OF THE engine and the back
and forth motion of the bus nearly rocked Sarah
to sleep. She sat in an aisle seat, looking past
Ian to the view out the window, trying not to let
her head droop onto his shoulder.

"Do we have a plan?" she asked.

"Basically, what you said the morning they
left. You tackle Liz and I'll tackle Mike."

"If they're around. Liz might have gone
home. Come to the hotel with me to see?"

"Sure."

"I'm already kind of missing our camp."

"You're not."

"No TV, no Internet, no telephone. Once you
get used to it—"

"I must have missed that, the part where you
got used to it."

"I *did*."

"Five minutes before the hunters found us?"

She smiled, caught. "Yeah. About that. Maybe

ten. There was an appeal to it, though, wasn't there? Getting back to basics." She nudged him. "Seeing what a tough guy you really are. He flies! He shoots! He cooks bunnies!"

He takes me to the moon and back. Honesty was all very well, but she couldn't tell him that.

The truck that had appeared out of nowhere had belonged to a group of Dene hunters who were following the caribou herd. It was luck their paths had crossed. Minutes either way, and they might have missed each other. A different decision by the caribou could have meant days more walking.

When Ian told the hunters about the bear and the long hike from Mike's camp, they were shocked.

"They left you?" one man had said, frowning. "Don't they know about the animals, the muskeg? It can suck you in. Blizzards can come, even in August. Minus fifty, and six feet of snow. It happens. Your friends were stupid."

Ian had nodded. "Which we're eager to tell them."

The men had driven Sarah and Ian back to their village and arranged a meal for them. A fishing boat had taken them along the river to a town with an all-weather road and bus service. Now, they were minutes from Yellowknife.

THE HOTEL MANAGER ASSURED Sarah he had continued to hold her room, even though her Barren Lands trip had taken longer than expected. Her friends, he added, still occupied the adjoining room. Thinking of the bill, Sarah almost wished she hadn't.

"Friends?" she repeated to Ian, in the elevator. "My company has company?"

"See what it feels like?"

"Did I apologize for that?"

"You don't need to."

"Because I'm sorry. Joining your trip when I knew you didn't want me to, inviting my author..."

"It's been entertaining."

The elevator opened at her floor. Entertaining? She'd tried to look at it that way, but really, the trip had stopped being entertaining the moment he'd looked up from the bar that first night.

Ignoring the tub, dimly visible through the open bathroom door, wasn't easy. Neither was walking past the high, duvet-covered bed. With Ian at her side, she knocked at the room's adjoining door.

After a few moments, Liz opened it, an expression of polite interest turning to one of astonishment and guilt.

"Shh," she said.

An odd beginning.

She came through into Sarah's room, closing the door behind her and didn't speak again until they'd all gone across to the desk.

"Are you all right? You don't quite look all right. How did you get here? Did Mike go back for you? He said it was too soon, but I didn't think so and Jack said—"

"Jack knows?"

"Shh," Liz repeated. "He's here. I couldn't very well go home while you two were still in the Barrens. But Rose isn't wild about hotels. It's been rough."

"Poor you."

"Are you furious?"

Sarah ignored the first few questions. "Are we furious, Ian?"

"Definitely."

"I'm so sorry. Really."

"If you'd thought about the wolves we heard at Marie camp," Sarah began.

Liz nodded, and kept nodding.

"The possibility of bears," Ian added.

"The lack of hot running water."

"The flies."

"Mosquitoes. The total and complete absence of hot running water."

Liz tilted her head at Sarah. "You don't actually sound all that furious."

"I was, I assure you. The first day I really castigated you, didn't I, Ian?"

"Oh, yeah."

"The second day, too."

"But then we settled in," Ian said.

Sarah nodded. "Made our peace with the situation."

"I was hoping you'd make your peace with each other."

"That was naive, Liz. Did you really think marooning two long-divorced adults in Bug Country would lead to a happy ending?"

"I guess I did."

"Unfortunately—and surprisingly, to you and me—life isn't a children's book. The beautiful princess wasn't rescued and the toad didn't change into a prince."

Ian pulled Sarah's shirt, backing her toward him. "What story were you reading? There wasn't any princess. There was only a brave and noble knight—"

Sarah gave an audible snort.

"—chopping through thorns to find the distressed damsel."

"If there was a damsel, and I'm not agreeing

there was, she certainly wasn't distressed and she certainly could have handled any thorns—"

"Please, you two," Liz said. "Don't start, okay? I'm sorry. We were trying to help. Obviously we should have stayed out of it. Sarah, why don't you take a shower, change your clothes? I'll order room service and then tell you what's happening here."

"Tell me now."

"It can wait. You're a bit smelly—"

"That's the price you'll pay."

"The total price?"

"Fair and square."

"Okay." Liz smiled, looking much too relaxed and confident for someone so recently let off the hook. "The first thing was that I found a sweet little bookstore in Old Town. The owner had already ordered copies of my next book! There's enough demand for it that they have a sign-up sheet. Imagine if you'd known about that—you would have been even more upset. Anyway, she and I had a wonderful visit and I arranged to do a reading when it comes out—"

"It?"

"My next book. Workshops with some early grades kids, too."

"Your next book? There's a book?"

"How could there not be, with you as my muse, berating me and urging me on?"

Ian said, "She dressed up as a Muse the other day…."

Liz went back to her room and returned with an armload of canvases.

"You've been painting?"

"A little."

A lot, Sarah thought. She recognized aspects of northern scenery as Liz arranged them on the bed, but they contained something more. Something about the way it felt to be so isolated, something about all the years the landscape had sat, undisturbed by humankind. She talked excitedly about the story that was beginning to percolate, about stones standing still, looking out at the sea, bound to the land while seals played and belugas arched out of the water, white as icebergs.

She must have noticed Sarah wasn't jumping up and down.

"It's all connected," she explained, "the beginning of our planet, rock and water meeting long before there were human eyes to see."

"It's fascinating," Sarah agreed. "But…I don't see how it's a children's story."

Liz stared at Sarah as if she was the least imaginative person she'd ever encountered.

Then she grabbed a pad of sticky notes from the desk, drew a quick sketch, turned to a new page and sketched again. She ripped off the two notes and stuck them on one of the paintings.

A house, with a reindeer outside.

A little girl in flannelette pajamas.

"Okay," Sarah said. "Do you mind doing that?"

"I can tell one story and suggest another." Liz began sketching again, attaching squares of paper to one canvas after another—a polar bear on an ice floe, a beluga with its great head and big, intelligent eyes lifting out of the water, an arctic tern circling overhead. "It's not exactly a spring story."

"We'll move it to fall."

"This isn't a plucky girl visits Toyland, right? When she finds Santa, the story ends. Maybe he invites her in for cocoa, but that's it. No elves, no sleigh ride home. This girl's an explorer. She finds her own way through life." Liz pointed to the scenery. "The magic's out there."

Her expression changed, warming and softening, when a man came through the adjoining door carrying a baby.

"Rosie's awake," he told Liz. "Good to see you again, Sarah." He nodded to Ian. "You survived my wife's misguided attempts at matchmaking?"

"Best holiday I've had in years."

After admiring Rose and hearing about Jack's decision to join his wife for a holiday, Sarah whispered to Ian, "My work here is done."

"Not mine. I have a story to file and an outfitter to confront. Dinner afterward?"

"We can meet at the Lair. Watch a football game." She could see that surprised him. Pleased him, too. "Be gentle with Mike, Ian. He helped Liz get to her story."

"A gentle uppercut? I'll try."

IAN FOUND MIKE AT THE floatplane base, tinkering with the Otter. It was almost funny watching the number of expressions that crossed his face in mere seconds. Almost.

"You're back!"

"A lot bitten and a little bit wiser."

"Sarah with you?"

With that casual question, Ian's anger surged through him, and for the first time in his life words, reason, nearly failed him. Fists seemed like really good tools.

"No, I left her out there. With the grizzlies. Of course she's with me."

"Mad, eh?"

Ian scratched a bite above his eyebrow,

another on the back of his neck, then beside his ear. That one was sore; the cartilage didn't leave much room for swelling. Most of the time he tried not to scratch, but he needed something to do until the urge to wallop Mike passed.

"I don't expect Liz to know better. She's not from here, and she's an artist. She thinks in pictures, in plots, in happy endings. But you. You know what can happen out there."

"I've camped in the Barrens plenty of times."

"Sarah hasn't."

"She had you. The conditions aren't so different around Churchill. I knew you'd take care of her. It was an opportunity for the two of you." In a rush, he added, "I mean, yeah, there were dangers. It was reckless, in a way. A measured risk. Did we leave you there long enough? Did you hash things out?"

The guy couldn't talk fast enough. No questions about how they'd get back to town though, no explanations of why the pick-up day had come and gone.

"Have you filed the papers?" Ian asked.

"Marie's claim?" Mike nodded. "Soon she'll be debt-free, worry-free and free to walk up the aisle."

"I thought I'd give you a chance to reconsider."

Mike laughed. He seemed to think Ian was

joking. "I've had five years to think about it! She's the woman for me."

"Unless you give her reason to doubt you."

Mike went still, except for a steady blinking. "There's no reason not to sell." He had decided to play innocent. "This is what she's been working for all these years. The big companies are falling over themselves for chances like this."

"Chances," Ian repeated. "That's what mining is all about, right? There aren't any guarantees."

Mike hastened to agree. "There aren't even guarantees with guarantees half the time. You find that out when your toaster breaks down."

"So if a company buys Marie's claim and it turns out to be a dud—" Ian broke off, shrugging.

Mike's shoulders went up, too. "Exactly. It's a gamble."

"Is that what you'd tell Sergeant Wainwright if he wanted to talk about it?" That got Mike's attention. Finally. Ian could see him measuring risk again. "Is it what you'd tell Marie? What would you tell either of them about stranded passengers?"

The last two questions seemed to shake Mike. Ian didn't think it was an act. Hard to make yourself pale on command. "You know what Sarah and I are most curious about?"

A faint shake of the head.

"Whether you planned to come back for us."

"God, yeah. Ian. Of course."

It sounded true. Ian's next move—an immediate call to the RCMP or giving Mike time to correct his actions—had depended on the answer. He waited, but all Mike did was stare out over the lake. He was quiet for so long Ian decided to leave him alone to think.

SARAH WAITED FOR IAN at the bar.

"Who is this shiny man?" she asked when he finally arrived. She leaned in to sniff his freshly shaved cheek. "Yum. Shaving cream is the best smell in the world. Column filed?"

"All done."

"Guess who called me?"

"Can't."

"Big, bad Mike."

Ian's face tightened with anger. "I don't like him bothering you."

"He was afraid to talk to you again, I think. He told me he was so, so sorry for the whole thing and that he was about to take an emergency trip to see Marie for an urgent meeting."

Ian nodded grimly. "Emergency and urgent, both. Good. He's catching on. I guess we'll wait and see if he does the right thing."

"Poor Marie. Hard times ahead."

They needed the comfort of chairs, not bar stools, so they moved to a table to order their meal. Ian enjoyed the cheeseburger and fries he'd craved out in the Barrens, but none of the sports on television could keep his attention.

"It's a dip in your adrenaline levels, I'll bet," Sarah said. "All that determination to get back safely and now here we are, the challenge over. It's a bit of an empty feeling."

"I don't think that's it."

Sarah didn't have any other suggestions, not ones she was willing to make. She knew what she was feeling. Her euphoria at being safe and clean was fading, because it was almost time to say goodbye.

Unless they didn't say goodbye.

After all they'd been through, didn't he know he was important to her? Did he have to hear it said? She had dropped everything, traveled for miles, two takeoffs and landings, searched hotels and bars, followed him into the Barren Lands, draped herself enticingly here, there and everywhere, and got into a fight with a grizzly.

Didn't he think all that meant something? What did he want from her before he'd say if he was willing to try again? *Did* he want to try?

She wasn't going to go first with any declarations or proposals.

"You're the best lover I ever had," she said, her voice as light as she could make it. "I'd give up coffee, silk, my balcony—and that's not nothing, Ian, that's my view of English Bay. I'd give up dark chocolate and ruby-red and all my rings but one for an occasional night with you."

"All but one?"

She reached under her top for the chain and pulled out the ring he'd given her twelve years ago. "That one. That's the keeper."

He still didn't say what he was thinking. She could leave it at that, pass it off as flirtation, or she could take a flying leap into the unknown.

"I love you, Ian. I never stopped."

Silence. Expressionless silence.

Was he embarrassed? Wondering how to let her down? She couldn't tell. That was the problem with declarations. Once they were made, they couldn't be retrieved. They sat there, abandoned, turning blue from lack of air. And the person hearing them had to deal with them one way or another. It was unfair, really, to hand someone else such an awkward task.

"I think we can agree there was a long and fairly definite pause," Ian said softly.

"We were done. Right? We gave up. I tried to stop loving you. I tried to love other people."

Oh, hell. She was going to have to go all the way with this. She needed to convince him it wasn't a game.

Tears came to her eyes. When she blinked them away, more came, faster. "There's no one else in the world I want but you. There's no one else who fits me the way you do. No other face in my mind, no other person I'm so afraid of hurting—"

He reached for her hand, kissed her fingers, then her palm. "Don't give up ruby-red, okay? Especially ruby-red silk. There are two rings I'd rather you found new owners for, but I wouldn't mind joining you on that balcony. Naturally, with coffee and chocolate. Both dark."

"Do you have any time frame in mind?"

"I was thinking starting now and going forever and ever."

For the first time in ten years every bit of tension left her. She felt as if she could float. "I love the thought of forever and ever."

"I'm kind of liking the idea of now, too."

"Now's good. Your room?"

Because they were so stiff and sore, they went upstairs slowly. They groaned getting out of their clothes and then, thankfully, burrowed into what felt like the biggest, softest bed in the world.

Ian unfastened the chain from around Sarah's neck and let the ring tumble into his hand.

"I can get you a better one now."

"No, you can't. Not if you owned every mine in the North and every jewelry store in New York City. You dropped History of Western Canada from 1879 to the Present for this ring. It's not going anywhere."

He reached for her hand. "Third finger, if you please."

She held it ready.

"With this ring I thee wed…."

"It's short notice, Ian, I don't have one for you."

She would have to improvise. She pushed him onto his back, raised herself over him and sank down. "With this…" She tightened around him, enjoying his quick intake of breath. "With this gesture of goodwill."

He laughed, soft and deep.

"Don't move." He paid no attention, so she re-phrased it. "Keep still. You're the recipient here."

His hands slid over her breasts. "Is this allowed?"

"Definitely. But that's all."

One hand snaked up her back, into her hair, and brought her head down for a kiss. "This?"

"No, no, no. I'm the doer."

"I'm the do-ee?"

"Is that so difficult?"

"Easiest thing in the—" He gasped when she pulled up and tightened, a move she owed to a belly dancing seminar. It took concentration, sore as all her muscles were, but she gave it her best, and he didn't talk anymore.

Soon she forgot about technique. She was aware of the way he filled her, of his heat, of the rippling that moved them and, strangely, even closed in his room, she was aware of a cooling north breeze, full of willow and Labrador tea.

EPILOGUE

IF THE BUZZER HAD WOKEN the baby, Sarah was going to be very upset. She peeked into the nursery, softening at the sight of the blue mound in the crib. Fingers curled, eyes shut tight, mouth pursed and sucking now and then, as if he was in the middle of a food-filled dream.

She closed the door and tiptoed back to the living room, where Ian stood with a small parcel.

"It was a courier," he said.

Sarah was less interested in the package than she was in the tea that must be just about perfectly steeped. Enjoying a cup from start to finish while it was still hot was a rare pleasure these days.

Wordlessly, she pointed to the teapot, then to the balcony. Conversation was like an alarm clock for the baby. Even at two months, he didn't like to miss anything.

Ian embarked on charades of his own,

pointing to her and then to a chair outside; to himself, the parcel, the pot, the tray, all his movements so emphatic, and accompanied by such active eyebrows, that she nearly ruined it all by bursting into laughter. He saw the risk and grabbed her, pushing her out to the balcony.

She watched him through the screen as he went from cupboard to fridge and back, finding cups and cream, the jam her mother had made from Whiteshell blueberries and brought to Vancouver on her first postbirth visit, and the scones his mother had baked and frozen during hers.

When they were seated outside, baby monitor on the table and cups in hand she said, "Go ahead. Open it."

"It's addressed to you. From Marie."

They hadn't heard from Marie since the wedding. Sarah lifted her cup and sipped the tea. It was exactly the strength and flavor she liked. She wasn't going to let it go cold. "It must be a baby gift."

Ian gave the box a careful shake. "I hear something moving. A rattle?" He unwrapped the brown paper. Inside was a birchbark box.

"It's beautiful," Sarah said. "Like the ones in the craft stores in the Old Town. How nice of her. We'll have to put it on a high shelf until we're sure he won't break it."

Inside the box was another container, a round one. Sarah leaned forward to see, distracted from her tea, after all. Ian lifted the lid, revealing a fabric pouch. It was the kind gem sellers used.

He handed it to Sarah. "You'd better take it from here."

She gently felt the contents through the cloth. Something hard and round and sharp. She loosened the drawstring and tilted the bag, shaking it.

Out rolled a ring. A beautiful ring, with what appeared to be two garnets on either side of a large diamond.

There was something else in the bag. Sarah drew out a piece of folded paper.

"An explanation?" Ian asked.

She began reading aloud. "'Hey, you two. Surprised?'" Sarah looked at Ian. "I think it's fair to say we are." He nodded, with a hell, yeah, expression, and she went back to the note. "'Six months ago I found a kimberlite pipe—'" Sarah broke off again, remembering to be quiet as she exclaimed, "Ian! She did it!"

"Does she say where she found it?"

"I don't think so. Let's see... 'An actual pipe with actual indicators. The garnets on your ring were cut from a couple of those. In the first core sample were two unusually large, flawless stones (which bodes well for the richness of the mine to come). The biggest one is on my finger, although Mike is disturbed that I provided my own engagement ring.'"

"Hey," Ian said. "That's great."

"'The second, smaller one forms the center of your ring, Sarah. Mike and I feel we played a part—in his case a very irresponsible part!—in your journey back to each other and that you and Ian played a compassionate and important part in keeping us together.'

"'You might feel this ring is too big a gift—' I certainly do '—but we ask that you accept it without hesitation. For two reasons, Sarah. As thanks, of course, but especially to mark the end of your two-year curse. We really weren't sure you could do it!!!' She put three exclamation marks after that."

"It deserves at least three, I'd say. And then a Hallelujah Chorus."

Sarah stuck out her tongue, but it was awkward to do while laughing. "There are a few more lines. 'The garnets represent years one and two of your second try with Ian. The diamond marks year three, the start of forever.'"

Her eyes misted as she reached the end of the note. The idea of forever was still new and precious. To see Ian's face each morning, to understand and be understood, to feel the comfort of familiarity and the surprise of discovery… She'd heard people claim they didn't regret anything in life because the many and varied pieces added up to make them who they were, but she wished she had always known how much fun it was, how satisfying, to grow and change together.

"What a generous gift," Ian said. "You all right, Sarah?"

"Too touched for my own good." She smiled, trying to lighten the mood and clear the lump out of her throat. "I wonder if she plans to mark our fourth and fifth anniversaries, too. If she keeps this up she'll need to give me a bracelet for our twenty-fifth. Twenty-five diamonds and garnets. Think how I'd sparkle."

Snuffling noises came from the baby monitor. "I'll get him," Ian said. "Once he's dry and fed we'll tell him the story of your ring."

"His ring, don't you think? He can give it to his bride."

She watched Ian go through the balcony door. The love of her life, her child's father. No wonder she'd been confused all those years ago. It wasn't a sunset they'd ridden into, after all. It was a whole new sunrise.

* * * * *